Treetime

by the same author

Albion's Dream

Treetime

Roger Norman

illustrated by Adam Stower

faber and faber
LONDON · BOSTON

For Katerina

First published in 1997
by Faber and Faber Limited
3 Queen Square London WC1N 3AU

Typeset by Faber and Faber Ltd
Printed in England by Mackays of Chatham plc, Chatham, Kent

All rights reserved

© Roger Norman, 1997
Illustrations © Adam Stower, 1997

Roger Norman is hereby identified as author of this
work in accordance with Section 77 of the Copyright,
Designs and Patents Act 1988

This book is sold subject to the condition that it shall not, by way of trade or otherwise, be lent, resold, hired out or otherwise circulated without the publisher's prior consent in any form of binding or cover other than that in which it is published and without a similar condition including this condition being imposed on the subsequent purchaser

A CIP record for this book
is available from the British Library

ISBN 0-571-17763-8

2 4 6 8 10 9 7 5 3 1

Contents

1 Scrabble, Scrabble 1
2 Midnight 9
3 The Hollow 14
4 On Wimble Toot 20
5 Daddy-long-legs 29
6 Mister Ash Comes In 36
7 The Red and White Army 43
8 Broad Oak 51
9 The Murk 57
10 Lonely Alder 65
11 Tricky Birch 77
12 The Fourteen Tribes 87
13 Bugging 103
14 The Attack 116
Afterword 128
More About Trees 134
Glossary 138

یکون جوابا

سید محمد محی الدین
مصطفی

1 Scrabble, Scrabble

The village was a long way from the town, the house was a long way from the village and the attic room was a long way from the rest of the house. Tonight was Alan's first night in his new room.

His old bedroom was too small now for both him and his sister, and he had grown out of the wallpaper, too, with its boats and toy trains. Emily had a whole menagerie of furry bears and spotted dogs and stripy cats, and Alan was too big for that sort of nonsense.

So he was moved to the attic where the ping-pong table lived, and where four large windows looked north, south, east and west. It was a twisting flight of stairs and a dark corridor away from anyone else. His mother kissed him goodnight and he looked at comics for a while. The water tank was in one corner of the room. From time to time it gurgled or groaned softly.

He turned off the light and was shocked at this strange place. Could it have changed so much? Was this really the same room where he had hopped about at the ping-pong table so many times?

Treetime

And that! What was that in the shadowy corner?

He froze. Something was there. Or somebody. He could see the hat, the head. Somebody was there in the corner, absolutely still and watching him. The important thing was not to move a muscle. If he didn't move, it seemed to him that whoever-it-was wouldn't move either.

The shadowy figure appeared to have something sticking out of the side of its head. Surely it was a large knife. Was the somebody dead then and simply propped up in the corner by the chair? Alan's eyes strove to see.

There was such a stillness about the figure that the boy became convinced that it was indeed a corpse, propped up. He thought now that he could hear something dripping on to the carpet.

But it wasn't a knife sticking out, it was the wrong shape. It was . . . the arm of the chair.

Suddenly, the figure was gone and there instead was the old wooden chair, with Alan's clothes thrown over it.

He turned on his bedside lamp. Sure enough it was the chair. The chairback had been the corpse's body. A bundled-up jersey flung over the top had been the person's ghastly head.

Yet the room still didn't look right. The water tank rumbled uncomfortably. The pool of light

Scrabble, Scrabble

cast by the bedside lamp was rather feeble as if it was losing the battle against the shadows.

Alan sighed and turned off the light. This was his new, grown-up room. He was going to like it. It was too big, too lonely, too dark, but he would stick it out and make the place his own. He turned over towards the wall and pulled the blankets closely around him. He wasn't a bit sleepy. He wished it was morning.

Then the sound at the window began. Of course it was not someone trying to get in. Of course it wasn't. But what was it? There were fingers running across the glass. A fumbling noise at the latch. Then silence.

Then again little fingers scrabbling. Something like an actual knock. The fumble at the latch. Then quiet again.

The attic was high above the ground. There was no balcony, nowhere to stand outside, nowhere to climb but the drainpipe. But something was at the window, there was no mistaking it. Could it be reaching down from above, from the roof? Was there perhaps something that lived in the roof and came out at night? Perhaps – and this thought was truly frightening – this something was in the habit of coming into the attic room by night.

The scrabbling came again, louder. There was a

Treetime

groan from the water tank. Two distinct knocks on the glass. Knock. Knock.

Did it know that he was in there? Yes, that was it. The creature knew he was there and was angry that there was a new occupant of the attic room. It wasn't trying to come in, it was out there, hanging down from the eaves, scrabbling and knocking, wanting to scare him.

He could imagine it clearly now. Thin, skeletal, with bony arms and long fingers. Something that lived unseen in roofs. Something full of a wicked dislike.

The odd thing was that the scrabbling and knocking had a rhythmical quality like eerie music. Scrabble, scrabble, scrabble, knock, knock. Scrabble, scrabble, scrabble, knock, knock.

And to this eerie music, Alan finally fell asleep.

He had been wrong about the roof-creature. There was nobody outside and the sound at the window was only a tree.

Yet he was not altogether wrong, because the tree in question was Mister Ash, and Mister Ash was waking up. Unbeknown to Alan or to Emily or to Alan's mother or to nearly every other human inhabitant of the planet, the trees were waking up.

Not that trees are ever entirely asleep. All their

Scrabble, Scrabble

lives a thousand tiny rootlets are feeding, a thousand little shoots are shooting, buds are budding, leaves are forming or falling, bark is stretching, sap is rising and slowly, slowly the crowns of trees are lifting up towards the sky.

But their lives are quiet and patient and they do not move around, except in Treetime.

Nobody knows how often Treetime comes. The old folks told stories of woods that moved and of single trees that disappeared. Ancient travellers have tales of meeting trees who'd left their homes and wandered here and there, but most men called these story-tellers liars and their stories simply dreams.

Yet Treetime comes and no one is aware, for all the world must sleep when trees awake. Everything else must sleep in Treetime.

So nobody knows when and nobody knows why, yet this Treetime, this time when Mister Ash was slowly waking up outside the attic room, there was a reason, whispered no doubt from root to root and murmured leaf to leaf, and the reason was this: the trees had heard that Old Friend Elm had gone.

Broad Oak was there and Silver Birch and Whispering Beech and Mister Ash and all the others, too: Sir Sycamore, the Chestnut cousins, Horse and Sweet, Weeping Willow and the thorns

Treetime

and little bushes but Old Friend Elm had disappeared. And that is why the trees awoke again and Mister Ash's noises at the window were more than simply music in the wind.

Mister Ash stood closest to the house. He was tall, hard and strong, and Mister Ash had no love for the house he stood against. He had been there before it. He had been young and fine and strong with three proud limbs that grew straight upwards from his trunk. But when the builders had arrived to clear the site and build the house, part of the youthful Mister Ash was in the way. First they had lopped off some smaller branches, and for a week Mister Ash had snarled silently at them; then more branches had been ripped and twisted and then, *then*, two men had come with a big saw and had sawn through his largest, straightest, proudest bough.

Mister Ash had never forgotten and never forgiven. His wood slowly rotted where the bough had been sawn off, and ants made a home at the spot and ate out the rotting wood; and where the finest bough of all had stood there was instead a hole that grew in size as the tree grew and remained there, where Mister Ash's very heart should have been.

You would have looked at Mister Ash growing by the lonely house and you would have seen the

Scrabble, Scrabble

tallest, thickest, strongest ash tree you have ever seen, but you would have had no idea that, in the middle of him, there was a cavernous hole that grew and grew.

That wasn't all. Much later, when Alan's family took the lonely house, they'd hung a swing from one of his branches.

A swing! An insult!

The ropes that held the swing squeezed and scored the branch, to and fro, to and fro. Some summer afternoons the swing would never stop. Alan or Emily would sit and swing for hours and hours, but mostly Alan. He was the one. And deep down in the thoughts of Mister Ash, there grew a hatred of the boy.

So when Mister Ash felt, as all the trees felt, that Treetime was coming, he saw the opportunity for revenge. At ten years old Mister Ash had been attacked with a saw. He had been lopped and twisted and deeply wounded, and the boy Alan was ten years old this Treetime.

A tree that lives close to people starts to think a little more in the human way. Lord Cedar, deep in the forest, knew nothing of men and cared less. His idea of Treetime was a deeply satisfying stroll around his realm. Treetime for the pines on the hill meant a trip to the southern coast to air themselves in the sea-breezes. But the trees that lived

Treetime

among men were different, and this Mister Ash lived closest of all.

So it was that when the first stirrings of Treetime came to Mister Ash – he felt it first in his root-ends and twig-tips – he thought of the boy. And his twig-tips told him that the boy was in the attic room.

Slowly, slowly as the boy was trying to sleep, Mister Ash leant and stretched towards the window.

No. The scrabble, scrabble, scrabble, knock, knock was not just the wind, it was the start of Mister Ash's campaign. When he felt the boy's fear, he chuckled deep inside his trunk.

2 Midnight

The next day was wet and stormy and Alan stayed indoors. Outside, the roots of the trees were slowly loosening in the heavy rain and a walker in the woods that day would have heard strange creaks and cracks as wooden muscles never used began to stretch.

Each tree had a different way of waking. Some of the smaller trees and shrubs would remain fast asleep until the very last moment and then suddenly, when midnight came, would shake themselves from crown to root-tip, like a dog after a swim, draw their roots from the soil and spring on to the surface of the ground.

Little Berry Elder could come awake with no more effort than it takes you to get out of bed in the morning, but for big trees like the ash and oak and beech and cedar it was more like getting up after a long illness, and they would spend a whole day gradually gathering their strength.

But Mister Ash had only one thought: to lean closer and closer to the attic window, smash it open and grab the boy.

So while Alan played that afternoon in his new

Treetime

room, the noises at the window grew louder and more frequent, but Alan just thought it was the storm.

His mother came to see him once and was surprised at the clattering outside.

'We must get those branches cut back tomorrow,' she said. 'Another storm like this and we'll have some broken panes.'

The ash twigs heard and told the tree, and Mister Ash grew a little quieter as evening drew on towards night, but his determination was greater than ever.

Now Mister Ash knew the laws of Treetime. Clocks stop, engines die and every living creature stays stock-still where it is. Yet not quite *every* creature. Anything that is in a tree when the trees awake at midnight gets caught up in Treetime, so Treetime is shared by a number of birds, a large army of beetles and woodlice and tree-dwelling ants and caterpillars, families of squirrels and bats, and anything else that happens to be lodged in a tree at that very moment.

But people asleep in their homes are safe, as if they are in another world. Imagine what might happen if it were not so! Mischievous Berry Elder could steal into homes – something he liked very much to do – and run away with sleeping babies, just for fun. Weeping Willow could sweep up girls and sing them songs so sad that they would never laugh again, and careless firs on cliffs could toss people like pebbles out to sea, and watch whose throw was furthest.

So what Mister Ash had to do was to have the boy in his clutches at the stroke of midnight.

Alan slept early that night. His chair didn't bother him by turning into ghastly shapes, and the noises at the window no longer worried him now that he knew what they were. He snuggled cosily down under the covers.

So he didn't hear, as the clock ticked on towards twelve o'clock, how these noises grew more frequent and louder still, as Mister Ash bent all his will towards the attic window.

'Further, further!' he urged his branches, and they in turn told the twigs and leaves.

If the wind hadn't helped, the task might have been beyond the power of Mister Ash, rooted as he still was, but the storm had grown fiercer and each time the wind gusted, it blew the twigs against the house.

At last, a few minutes before twelve, a particularly wild gust drove a bunch of larger branch-ends on to the window, a pane smashed, the latch snapped and the window flew open.

Alan woke with a start and switched on his bedside lamp. The wind was inside the room, picking up papers and flinging them about. Broken glass lay scattered on the floor and the window was banging crazily.

'Only the storm,' Alan told himself and went to the window to close it. But as he struggled to do so, he realized that too much of the tree had blown in through the opening and that the window would not now shut.

He began trying to bundle the branches back outside with one hand and force the window closed with the other. And it was then that he had the odd feeling that the twigs were clutching at him, clinging to his arm. He let go of the window, and thrust both hands against the mass of twigs and leaves.

There seemed to be more of the tree inside the window than before and the boy found himself fighting against an armful of struggling foliage. The more he pushed it away, the more it seemed to come back at him. He could feel the pricking and rasping of the twigs against his hands and arms and he shied away as they began to claw at his face.

It was at this moment that midnight struck and all the clocks stopped.

Then it was another world. People in bed slept peacefully on, but in one house not far away a man reading late abruptly froze, his hand reaching out to turn the page. In another house, a woman stirring a pot stopped in mid-stir, and a kitten rubbing itself against the woman's legs was suddenly still as a statue. Even the flames of the gas ring ceased their restless dance and stood motionless in a small circle of blue.

The rain stopped, and the wind, too. The bell that chimes the hour on the church tower in the village chimed once and was silent. The last train from the coast drew to a shuddering halt in the middle of nowhere. A mouse was scurrying across the road one minute and the next was like a little stone in the middle of the way. A fox out hunting stood stuck astride a ditch.

But the trees were on the move. Berry Elder was up in a trice and started to dance. Broad Oak heaved himself mightily upwards and with one great surge was free. Whispering Beech seemed to gather herself smoothly and gracefully, as a woman might gather the folds of her dress, and glided from the spot she had occupied for so long. Silver Birch spun round and round before springing swiftly into the air.

Squirrels rippled down trunks and ran away to hide. Birds started from their perches and flew away to seek safer spots. Idle bats took to their wings.

Only the trees liked Treetime.

3 The Hollow

And what of Mister Ash?

Mister Ash was not stout and rugged like Broad Oak, nor was he slender and graceful like Whispering Beech, nor young and quick like Berry Elder. He impatiently tore up his roots and when he began to move it was an awkward business at first, as if he was propelling himself on rusty roller-skates.

But inside him was a smile of grim pleasure, for high up in his branches, trapped in a prickly embrace, was a terrified young boy who wriggled and squirmed but who, with every wriggle and every squirm, found himself more thoroughly entangled and more tightly held.

It was no longer night but there was a greyish light like early dawn. The storm was over but no birds sang and no cocks crowed.

This is a dream, Alan thought, and felt better. A dream, of course. He was safely in bed and he had only dreamt that the window had been flung open and the branches had grabbed him.

Then he saw the other trees and caught his breath. The elder was dancing, a couple of large

The Hollow

oaks were riding off towards the hill beyond the garden. Even the bushes of the hedge had broken ranks and were moving away in small groups. There was a scattering of apples on the lawn but no apple tree now stood above them. Further off, the wood was slowly shifting, like a pattern in a kaleidoscope. A band of pines was marching to the cliffs.

As he stared in amazement, Alan stopped struggling, and this was what Mister Ash had been waiting for. More branches closed in on the boy, and he suddenly found himself being grabbed from all sides and forced down towards the middle of the tree.

Again he began kicking and struggling, but the branches were stouter now and there were too many of them. He was nudged and knocked and tumbled and dragged downwards.

Then he saw the hollow for the first time, right below him. It looked as if it had opened up specially to swallow him.

He got a leg free, put it against the branch below him and pushed upwards with all his strength. But all he got for his pains was a sharp rap on the head that nearly knocked him senseless.

Two big branches squeezed him now and a cluster of smaller boughs above him pressed him downwards. Bark scraped his legs and his tracksuit was ripped.

The hollow was only just beneath him, and when the two big branches suddenly let go, he dropped a short distance and slid straight into the opening. A small stout branch that grew at the fork instantly bent over to plug the gap above him.

Inside the hollow it was dark and damp and there was a strong smell of moss and wet bark. Alan was scratched and bruised yet he was strangely unafraid. He was just glad to be out of the clutches of the branches.

He found himself sitting in a small moss-lined chamber and, as his eyes grew accustomed to the gloom, he saw that the faint light was not only coming in from the top, where the stout branch stood guard, but also from a narrow slit just above the level of his head. By craning upwards he could see outside. It was a bit like being in the gun-turret of a tank.

Mister Ash was on the move. Every now and then there was a bump, and once the whole tree lurched and Alan was thrown against the wall of the hollow, but soon they were coasting along evenly enough.

When they reached the ditch where the hedge at the bottom of the garden had stood only a short while before, Alan braced himself and was startled to feel the tree leap into the air to clear the ditch. They landed with a jolt, bounced a couple of times and rolled smoothly on.

By getting on to his hands and knees Alan was able to keep his eyes to the slit. The tree didn't have much foliage at that point, and he had a good view of what was happening in front of them. It was an astonishing sight.

Not a single tree or bush was still. Berry Elder overtook them, bouncing merrily along as if on springs. Some slender pines sped by like skaters on ice. A bevy of small thorns was ahead, bunched closely together, stopping and starting briskly off again then stopping once more. A kind of buzzing arose each time they stopped and Alan had the impression that they were arguing among themselves. Many of them had obviously been part of hedges and they looked funny with their tops and two of their sides trimmed close, giving them an elongated appearance, like people with very peculiar haircuts.

Further off, other trees were on the move and they seemed to be making for a small hill in the middle of a large meadow. It was a place where Alan had been often enough, but all the countryside was so completely changed that it was difficult to work out where everything should have been. Woods and copses and hedges had disappeared, and there were trees where there had never been a tree before.

He wondered again whether he was dreaming. It was the only explanation, yet somehow it didn't feel like a dream. There didn't seem to be any of those odd shifts and gaps that dreams always have.

'No dream,' said a voice.

Alan froze.

'Definitely no dream,' said the voice again, and there was a deep, throaty chuckle.

At first Alan thought that the voice came from somewhere below him, then it seemed to be coming from the walls of the hollow itself.

'Who's there?' he asked nervously.

'Peculiar question. Who else but me? Who else could it be but me?' The words came in short clammy puffs like warm breaths on a frosty day.

'Who are you?' Alan asked, looking quickly this way and that.

'Mister Ash, of course. I am all around you. You are in my special place, for keeping things like you.'

'*Keeping* things?'

'Yes. Keeping for a short keeping. Or keeping for a very very long keeping.'

'But what do you want me for? Why did you

The Hollow

grab me? Why didn't you leave me alone?'

Suddenly Alan realized that the little chamber was not so much like a gun-turret as a prison.

'Yes,' the voice went on. 'Just like a prison.'

Alan was sure he hadn't spoken his thoughts aloud. Could the tree read his mind?

'Indeed I can. Easy for an old ash to read a little empty head like yours. Very easy.'

'Well, stop it!' said Alan angrily. 'Stop reading my head.'

Again the throaty chuckle.

It was a horrible idea. He was a prisoner, he could understand that. There was a hollow and a stout branch on guard and a slit that looked out and he was stuck inside – all this he could somehow accept. But that the ash could hear his every thought, that even his thoughts were not his own, that was truly frightening.

'Yes. Every single thought. Oh yes,' came the moist, vaporous voice.

'*Stop that*!' shouted the boy again.

4 On Wimble Toot

Alan had been right, for there was to be a meeting on the little hill. It wasn't really a hill but more a large bump or tump in the middle of a flat piece of land. Alan remembered that people called it Wimble Toot, though what on earth a 'toot' was, he hadn't a clue.

When Mister Ash climbed the short slope to the top of Wimble Toot, there were already quite a few trees there before him. Looking out, Alan could see the thorns, still buzzing, and Silver Birch standing to their left. Opposite them were a magnificent beech and a giant oak. Alan recognized this oak as one that normally lived on the edge of the big wood. He was sure that there couldn't be another one quite so huge in the vicinity.

There was also a sycamore and a fine cedar, a pine, the little elder and other trees that the boy did not immediately recognize. There were about a dozen trees in all, standing more or less in a circle.

A strong, rough voice spoke up. 'Welcome to the First Clock. Are we one of every kind?'

'We are, Broad Oak,' replied another voice.

'I, Oak, will talk of our task,' said the oak. 'It is to seek Old Friend Elm. All here may speak, but none shall call out or clamour. There must be no tricks or larks or pranks.' Broad Oak, it seemed, liked the sound of k's. When he said his k's he gave them a real *kick*.

Alan felt a stirring in Mister Ash, as if he wanted to say something. 'Always Fat Oak first,' he heard the tree murmur moistly.

But nobody heard this apart from Alan, and it was the thorns who made the next speech. There were five of them and they spoke in turn, as if they had one mind between them.

'Old Elm has been poisoned,' said the first in an angry, prickly voice.

'And cut down and chopped up,' continued the second.

'And carted away and burnt,' said the third.

'Or left to die and to rot,' went on the fourth.

'And it's all the doing of Man!' finished the fifth.

It was the turn of the first again.

'People must be punished!'

'We must harass their houses.'

'And gut their gardens.'

'And fling away their fences.'

'And smash their smart little cars.'

Treetime

Alan noticed that the five thorns were each slightly different. Three of them had that odd shape that came from living in hedges, and Alan wondered whether it was their haircuts that made them so angry. As they became more excited, they all began to speak at once in a loud, fierce buzz and only the odd word could be heard. Words like scratch, rip, ruin, bust and break.

'No clamouring and no mucking about,' came Oak's stern voice.

The thorns fell silent and the lofty beech started to rustle and sway as if a wind blew through her. Her voice was a whisper, like a gentle breeze. There seemed no effort in it, yet Alan heard every word.

'Listen close, my friends,' she whispered. 'Listen close and listen still. Listen to the sounds that travel in the air. Sounds of peace and patience, whispers of forgotten things, words of long-gone dreams, songs of long-gone streams. Listen carefully to these, my friends, listen bark, listen branches, listen leaves. Sounds of peace and patience, sounds of quiet ease. I pray for peace, my friends. Listen to me, please.'

As she spoke the last words she made a sweeping movement of her branches, pointing to the fields and hills and valleys around them. And many of the trees on the Toot seemed to nod in agreement.

On Wimble Toot

Berry Elder couldn't keep still. He was between the oak and the beech and, as if to make up for his lack of size between these two huge trees, he hopped restlessly here and there and once or twice leapt into the air. When one of the great trees was speaking, he moved so that he was directly underneath it and leant his slim trunk backwards, looking up and nodding energetically.

Now he spoke up, in a breathless, high-pitched chatter, apparently starting in the middle of a sentence, ' . . . may very well be right in what she says, for we must be careful in our dealings with men with their axes and saws and instruments of destruction and their greed for the timber of all the fine big trees like Broad Oak and Whispering Beech and the swift pines, and if men wake up after Treetime to find their houses ruined and their gardens gone it's my bet that there'll be trouble for us, so I say . . .'

It seemed there would be more, but Berry Elder finished as he had begun, in the middle of his sentence.

'Hear! Hear!' said Sir Sycamore.

Then it was Mister Ash's turn, and the chill, vaporous sound of his voice slid around Alan's cell.

'Cowardly thoughts,' Ash began. He paused, and his words hung in the air for a moment like a sudden fog.

Treetime

Nobody likes to be called a coward, least of all Broad Oak, who stiffened at the insult, sending a tremor through his hundred thousand leaves.

'Cowardly trees who too long have lived with birds and winds,' went on Mister Ash. 'Cowards who fear these tiny little people. Cowards with hollow trunks and swollen galls and brittle twigs. Sapless trees afraid of storms.'

All the trees were listening to him carefully. Lord Cedar cleared his throat but said nothing.

'Ash, at least, is not afraid,' continued Mister Ash's smazy, drisky voice. 'War is the answer and Ash will make war.'

The five thorns buzzed proudly next to their important ally and shifted a little to be closer to him.

'Hear! Hear!' said Sir Sycamore.

'Why should people sleep safely?' asked Mister Ash. 'Rooted and voiceless and powerless, we watch them prune and chop. Rooted and voiceless and powerless while they tread our little saplings underfoot. And now we will do the same to their little ones.'

These last words were especially chilling to Alan as he squatted in his prison. He alone knew that Mister Ash's campaign had already started, with him. He had a sudden desire to shout out to all of them, to let them know that he was there, and to tell them about their friend Elm who was dead. To tell them that it was not men who had killed the elms but only a beetle . . .

'Don't you dare speak!' Ash's words rushed on the boy from all sides. 'One word, one shout, and I'll crush you. Just one.'

Alan had forgotten. Even his thoughts weren't safe.

Outside, the debate continued. It was not only the thorns who ranged themselves on the side of Mister Ash. The pine took his part and so did Silver Birch.

Alan was surprised at this. He had always liked Silver Birch with her special white bark that peeled off so satisfyingly, like delicate paper. But he saw now that Silver Birch was more mysterious than he had thought. There was a lazy, eerie quality to her voice that was a little sinister and, as she started to speak, Alan noticed that she was surrounded by a band of red and white spotted toadstools that stood in a circle around the base of her trunk.

When she spoke, it was in a slow sing-song rhyme that made you listen whether you wanted to or not.

> *'Treekind listen to my song,*
> *Ash is right and Beech is wrong,*

Treetime

> *Trees have suffered far too long,*
> *Men have weakened what was strong.'*

'Hear! hear!' said Sir Sycamore. Lord Cedar cleared his throat but said nothing.

> *'Once this land was full of trees,*
> *Forest and woodland and thicket and copse,*
> *Grove and spinney and dell.*
> *With axes and chainsaws and greed and disease,*
> *Men chop and they rip and they rot and they fell,*
> *They do what they want and they take what they please.'*

The thorns buzzed with approval. 'Well said, Birch,' Alan heard Mister Ash mutter to himself.

> *'Time to put an end to their axes and saws,*
> *We've lain long enough in their roofs and their floors,*
> *Time to put aside the old oak-laws . . .'*

'Not oak-laws but the code of all our kind,' growled Broad Oak.

> *'Tree-nymphs danced and wood-dryads spoke*
> *In the days before beech, before pine, before oak,*

On Wimble Toot

*Once people knew of the magic spell
Of forest and thicket and spinney and dell.
But they thought and they think that the
    magic has fled,
They thought and they think that trees are
    just dead,
Men forgot tree-magic, and most trees forgot,
But myself, as for me, Silver Birch, I DID
    NOT!'*

She was speaking more and more slowly towards the end, more and more dreamily, as if she was lulling everyone to sleep. Then she shouted the last three words, *'I DID NOT!'* and everybody was wide awake again.

And Alan was astonished to see that the red and white toadstools that ringed the birch's trunk were growing before his very eyes. Their stalks grew longer, their caps unfurled and the white spots swelled like something on the surface of a balloon.

'Make magic,' chanted Silver Birch. A kind of lazy shiver shook her from base to crown, and all at once the toadstools were slipping swiftly and silently across the clearing towards Broad Oak.

Oak saw them coming, but before he could get his colossal bulk moving, the faerie ring of toad-

Treetime

stools was all around him and he was trapped in Silver Birch's spell.

5 Daddy-long-legs

There was something tickling Alan's ear. He had felt it before and had brushed it away, thinking it was a dangling thread of bark or a spider's web, but now he heard a sound as well, a faint whirring sound.

He turned to see what was there and as he did so, an insect landed on his nose.

'Hey!' he said, brushing it off.

'Don't brush people off without finding out who they are,' said a voice.

The voice was most certainly not that of Mister Ash. Alan drew back in surprise, looking for whatever had landed on him.

'Who are you?' he said. 'And where are you?'

'I'm right here in front of you.'

The voice wasn't loud but Alan heard the words clearly enough. It was as if there was a tiny radio somewhere close.

It was dark inside the hollow. Alan peered around him.

'Here in the light,' said the voice.

And there, perched on the lip of the opening and silhouetted against the light coming from

Treetime

outside, was a daddy-long-legs.

'You? Is it *you* talking?'

'Yes. Me. Why be surprised? Trees are moving, you are trapped in a hollow tree trunk, time has stopped and a so-called daddy-long-legs talks.'

The insect spoke rather impatiently.

'I'm sorry. I never thought of bugs talking.'

'There's a lot you never thought of. I bet you've never thought of *bugs* much at all.'

'Well no, not much.'

It was true. He liked ladybirds and found beetles and earwigs rather interesting. And only the other day he'd found a huge spider sitting in front of the garden roller and had decided to squash it under the great iron wheel. He had heaved the machine forward and watched as the spider got caught, leg by leg, until it disappeared under the roller. After a moment he had pulled it away again and stared as the spider drew itself horribly out of the flattened grass, like a monster coming forth from a marsh. He had even felt a little frightened as if the big spider was capable of some terrible revenge. Then he had stamped on it, again and again.

'I expect you would simply have squashed me if I hadn't spoken up,' said the tiny voice.

'No, I wouldn't actually,' said the boy quickly.

'I bet you would.'

'No, not you. Not a daddy-long-legs.'

'Why not?'

'I sort of like daddy-long-legs.'

A surprisingly loud laugh greeted this remark. Again Alan had the impression of listening to a small radio, as if what he was hearing was not in fact a voice but a transmission.

'You sort of like daddy-long-legs, do you? Why?'

Alan tried to think why. It was true that he regarded most bugs as suitable for squashing, especially in the house. But a daddy-long-legs was different. He wasn't sure why. He found them in the basin in the bathroom sometimes, or clumsily hurling themselves against the window trying to find a way out. And for some reason he helped them escape.

'Maybe it's because you're not very . . . clever,' he explained cautiously.

'It's you that isn't very clever,' said the daddy-long-legs sternly. 'Have a closer look at me and see if I'm *clever* or not.'

Alan leant closer to study the curious insect. He'd never really looked at one sitting still before. They always seemed to be whirring around like wounded helicopters. He had no idea that there was so much to them. Six very long legs as thin as the strands of a cobweb and each with a little suction pad as a foot. A narrow twig-like body with intricately patterned and wafer-thin wings. And a bewildering variety of antennae, two apparently in the middle of its back, two reaching out in front between the little black eyeballs and a cluster of tube-like things which protruded behind its front legs. It all looked very clever indeed, more like a miniature spacecraft than a bug.

'What are all these bits for?' asked Alan.

'Some whirr, some hum, some flutter. Some receive signals and some send signals out. Some see, some sense and some dance. Some feed and some fornicate.' The daddy-long-legs paused. 'Look out. Things are on the move outside.'

Alan had quite forgotten what was happening on the Toot. He put his eyes to the slit again. After the gloom of his prison, the light was blinding.

Broad Oak was still where he had been, surrounded by the toadstools, but the rest of the trees were leaving the meeting. The thorns and Silver Birch had already gone. Lord Cedar was to be seen striding off towards the wood. Mister Ash himself seemed to be waiting for something.

Whispering Beech had gone up to where Broad Oak was trapped. She was speaking to him in her breezy voice and her words seemed to rustle softly through the air as before.

'We have heard words of war. We have seen

Treetime

buzzing thorns and mushroom magic, a rash ash, a birch with mischief in mind; it's the wrong way of mourning our Old Friend Elm, a wrong way of warning humankind. I'll tell the tales of peace and I'll sing the songs of calm, my leaves have ever blessed the wind and my eyes have sought the sky, and this is no time for such as I. It is you, brother Oak, who must lead us now, so summon your strength and shake off the spell. Make haste, make haste.'

As she spoke she leant over towards Broad Oak and Alan saw how much taller she was than he.

Oak answered but his voice was very drowsy, as if he had difficulty keeping himself awake.

'Seek news of the unlucky elms. Keep an eye on the prickly thorns. Look out for Silver Birch's tricks. I'll come when I can.'

Alan wondered why Whispering Beech didn't just trample the ring of toadstools that held Broad Oak in thrall. But he was to learn why later.

Whispering Beech swayed slightly, as if nodding in reply, and swept off.

'The other trees have gone to destroy my house,' Alan muttered. And he had a sudden, awful picture of his home smashed to pieces by the angry thorns, and of his mum and Emily buried under the ruins of the house.

But the daddy-long-legs knew better.

'No, not yet,' he said. 'That was the first meeting. Clock, as they call it. There'll be a bigger meeting later – the Great Clock. Oak and Beech persuaded them that nothing should be done until then.'

Alan was puzzled.

'How do you know?' he said.

'Because I've been listening. I'm caught up in Treetime just like you, but unlike you I've been taking notice of what's going on.'

'But you were talking to me.'

'I've been listening to them as well.'

'How on earth could you do that?'

'I told you. I've got a number of devices for listening with.'

'You mean that you can listen to more than one conversation at once?'

'Several. While you and I have been talking, not only have I been listening to the events at the Clock, I've been keeping track of Mister Ash's plans as well.'

'That's amazing!'

'Yes. So next time you help a daddy-long-legs out of the bathroom window, don't do it because we're stupid. Right?'

'All right,' said Alan.

'I've got bad news for you as well,' continued the daddy-long-legs. 'Look above you.'

6 Mister Ash Comes In

Alan looked above him to see nothing but darkness. This was strange, for there should have been some light coming in from the top of the hollow. But there wasn't.

The mass of twigs and leaves that blocked the opening had grown thicker, and certain branches seemed to be reaching down inside the chamber itself. Cautiously, Alan explored with his hand. Wherever his hand touched a twig, he felt it clutching at him with its coarse little fingers.

'Yes,' said the daddy-long legs. 'Mister Ash is coming in.'

He was. Alan could hear the rustling and jostling above him as the branches and leaves squeezed themselves through the opening.

The boy began to fight back. They were only twigs after all, and twigs can be snapped.

But he couldn't stand up. He could only wave his arms wildly above his head, grabbing handfuls of leaves and twigs and tearing at them. He managed to break off a few twigs and a flurry of leaves, but the twigs were live and green and mostly they just bent under his grasp.

Mister Ash Comes In

Somewhere above him would be the big branch that was father to all these little branchlets. If only he could snap *that* one . . .

He stretched up as high as he could and thrust his hands upwards through the foliage, searching for the stout branch. Yes, there it was. He got one hand round it and reached up with the other.

But as he did so, he felt the twigs closing on him, scrabbling at his face, his neck, his shoulders. Sharp twig-ends dug into his flesh and one slender shoot seemed to be coiling itself around his neck.

And the stout branch was too stout. He heaved at it for a moment then let go and tried furiously to free himself from the clutches of the foliage. Finally he sunk to the floor of his prison, exhausted.

There was nothing he could do.

'You're a bit like a daddy-long-legs trying to find the way out of the bathroom window,' said the little static voice by his ear.

Alan felt tears come to his eyes.

'I'm stuck,' he choked. 'It's going to crush me.'

'Be still, little man,' said the daddy-long-legs. 'Catch your breath. It's not over yet. What you've got to do is *think*.'

'What do you mean, think?! I can't get out at the top. I can't get out anywhere,' said the boy, wildly.

Treetime

'What you need is a plan.'

'There isn't any plan.'

'It's you against the ash. Right?'

'Yes,' Alan sniffed.

'And the first rule of any battle is to know your enemy. So what do you know about Mister Ash?'

'He hates people. He's old and . . . and strong. He can move his branches and make them grow. He hates *me*. He wants to kill me.'

'What else?'

'Nothing. I don't know anything. There's something called Treetime. Perhaps . . .' Suddenly the boy saw hope. 'Perhaps it's all a dream and I'm going to wake up. Perhaps if I curl up and close my eyes, I'll wake up in my own bed.'

'That's not thinking. That's just imagining. Dreams aren't like this, are they? Dreams flit and change shape and dart around. No, it's not a dream, believe me. But there's something else you know about Mister Ash.'

'Well, he can talk.'

'Yes. And . . . ?'

'He can hear. And he can even read my mind.'

'Good. He can read your mind. That's where you must begin.'

'But what's the point in a plan? He'd know it immediately. He's probably listening to us now.'

'I'm sure he is, and that's probably why he's

Mister Ash Comes In

halted his attack for the moment, but the thing is that he can only hear *you*.'

'What about you?'

'Oh no. He can't hear me. I see to that.' The daddy-long-legs chuckled. 'He can only hear what you're saying and thinking. And if you've ever heard just one end of a telephone conversation, you'll see that it won't make much sense to him. He'll be a bit puzzled at the moment, will Mister Ash.'

Alan pondered this for a moment.

'But why can't he hear you as well?'

'Because I'm equipped with a sort of scrambling device. It's one of those extensions of mine that you were looking at. Oh yes,' finished the daddy-long-legs proudly, 'there's not much in the way of transmitting and receiving that I can't manage.'

The rustling, jostling noises started again as Mister Ash started to come further in. More foliage was pressing into the hollow and the boy made himself as small as he could to keep his head out of the way of the grasping twigs.

'Quick!' he shouted. 'Daddy-long-legs! What can I do?!'

'The tree reads your thoughts,' said the little voice quickly. 'So give him thoughts to make him stop.'

'But what?'

'Anything. Think how sorry you are. How right he is. But remember that you must not have any thoughts except the ones you want him to hear. And whatever you do, don't let him know that you are trying to trick him. Now. You must start *now*.'

Alan fought back his feeling of panic and started to think.

I'm very sorry to have offended you, Mister Ash, he thought. You are a great tree and I'm only a boy. I don't know why you hate me so much. Really I'd like to be your friend.

There was a silence in the hollow. Mister Ash was listening.

Alan thought desperately on.

This is no plan, he made himself think. This is the truth. I've always liked trees. In fact I've always liked the ash by the house. I never meant him any harm. Why do you hate me, Mister Ash? I never cut you or hurt you or laughed at you. I only . . . I only liked to swing on you, he thought.

And immediately there was that slight creaking, brushing, scurrying sound as more of Mister Ash's twigs and leaves crowded into the space above the boy's head, so Alan hurried his thoughts quickly on, hurrying so that no unwanted, secret thought should come into his head to

Mister Ash Comes In

give the game away, hurrying to stop this awful invasion of his little cell.

But now I realize, he thought, that I should never have used that stupid swing. How horrible it must have been for you, day after day. Yes, hour after hour, up and down, up and down, twisting your skin and scraping your bark. And I'll never, ever, ever use the swing again if you'll only let me go.

Now Mister Ash spoke, in his chilly, moist, misty way.

'Yes. The swing. Up and down, up and down. But now it's you that can't move, and me that can. And for you it's down and down, down and down.' His laughter was like the last of the bathwater disappearing down the plug hole.

Alan felt the twigs above him stirring again. He had to get out, get out, *get out*!

'You want to get out, little boy, do you?' came Mister Ash's voice. 'Oh no, you must find out what it's like not to be able to move. Feel what it's like to be stunted and twisted and . . .'

'If you let me out, I'll untie the swing.'

There was a silence that grew longer and longer.

'If I don't untie it for you,' Alan went on quickly, 'it'll always be there. Always. Knocking against your trunk. Twisting round your branch.

Treetime

Until the day you die.'

Another silence.

'But if I do let you out,' said Mister Ash, 'how do I know you'll keep your word?'

'You can read my thoughts, can't you? So you must know whether I'll do it or not.'

The truth was that there was nothing further from Alan's mind than to double-cross Mister Ash, and Mister Ash knew it.

'All right,' he said finally.

The trouble was that the ash could read Alan's thoughts, but Alan had no idea at all about the intentions of Mister Ash.

7 The Red and White Army

The light began to filter in above Alan's head once more as Mister Ash started withdrawing his branches from the hollow. The boy didn't wait for him to finish. Twigs scratched his face but he didn't care. For a moment he hung wriggling and kicking as he pulled himself up, and then he was through the gap and in the open air.

The swing hung from one of the broad branches above him. He climbed quickly up and edged along the branch, one leg on either side of it, until he got to the rope.

Lucky his mother couldn't see him now! He was high above the ground as he sat astride the branch and tugged at the knots. They had been drawn tight by the endless pulling of the swing and sodden by a hundred rainstorms. Alan's fingers began to ache but he stuck at his task. He didn't notice how the smaller branches above him were bunching together and reaching down towards him as he worked.

At last the first knot came free and one end of the rope snaked to the ground far below. The second one seemed a bit easier and it wasn't long

Treetime

before that one too began to come loose.

But the branches waiting above his head were too eager. Before the second knot was quite undone, a cluster of smaller branches clawed at Alan's back and grasped at his tracksuit. Suddenly the boy realized what they were up to. Mister Ash was planning to pop him back in the hole.

He forgot the narrowness of the branch he sat on. He forgot the ten-metre fall beneath him. With both hands he struggled against the branches that grasped him.

As he tore himself free, he lost his balance and felt himself falling. He lunged out desperately to grab on to something and his hand found the rope. At first he couldn't hold it. It slipped through his fingers, burning him, then he held on, swinging crazily from one hand.

The knot tightened again and held.

He got his other hand to the rope and began slithering downwards. His hands were on fire, but he was on the ground.

As he scampered to safety beyond the circle of Mister Ash's branches, he felt the tree starting to move behind him. But the boy was too quick for the lumbering old ash and only when Alan was well away did he risk a look over his shoulder at his pursuer. The danger wasn't yet over. The tree

The Red and White Army

was moving swiftly after him, leaping rather than rolling, and each leap seemed longer than the one before.

Alan found that he had run down the slope of the Toot and half-way around its base. There above him stood the immense and reassuring figure of Broad Oak. The boy ran back up the slope, skipped over the circle of red and white toadstools and up to the trunk of the tree itself. When he got there he turned again and there was Mister Ash, just beyond the toadstools.

'Broad Oak! Broad Oak!' shouted the boy.

But there was no reply.

Alan hammered on the trunk and shouted again, and as he did so he looked up and caught his breath at the sheer size of the tree that was spread out above him. There were three or four boughs that were themselves as thick as the trunks of a large tree.

'There's no help to be had from the oak,' Mister Ash called out. 'Treetime's finished for Fat Oak.'

But Mister Ash made no move to approach the boy where he stood under the colossal branches. Instead, and to Alan's great relief, Mister Ash turned to go.

'I'll be seeing you,' he called out. 'By your house, I expect, or *what's left of your house.*'

Treetime

As Mister Ash rolled away across the fields, Alan could see the swing bumping along behind him.

Broad Oak seemed to be fast asleep, caught in the spell of the toadstools. Alan sat at the foot of the great tree for a while, with his back against the trunk. Once he got up and strode all the way round, counting the paces. Fourteen.

But when he sat down again he found himself feeling suddenly weary. This was natural enough. After all, he'd hardly slept that night.

And yet it wasn't natural. It didn't *feel* natural. It was like a heavy curtain being lowered in his mind. It was as if something other than sleep was closing his eyelids . . .

Abruptly the boy opened his eyes and forced himself to his feet. How stupid he had been! He started running out of the sinister circle, but somehow his legs wouldn't do what he wanted. He tripped and nearly fell, then stumbled on again. Ground, sky, branches and fields spun dizzily about before his eyes. He ran a few steps more but a moment later he came smack up against the oak's trunk.

He turned so that the trunk was behind him and, with his eyes tightly closed to keep out the sickeningly spinning world, lurched forward, with his arms flung out in front of him.

The Red and White Army

But it was like being on a merry-go-round that was going too fast and he kept being pulled back towards the centre.

He dropped on to his hands and knees and began to crawl. He opened his eyes now and made them look at the ground immediately in front of him. Step by step he dragged himself towards the edge of the faerie circle. The desire to sleep was almost overpowering.

At last, almost between his hands, there was one of the toadstools. It seemed to have grown. In fact it seemed to be swelling before his very eyes. It was like a huge red balloon with white patches that shifted and danced. There was something beautiful about it, the dance of the white shapes on the deep red background, something mesmerizing.

The toadstool had grown so much that it occupied his whole vision. Wherever he looked, it was there in front of him. He got up and tried to push it out of his way. It turned in his hands like a great globe.

But now he got angry at this spinning, swelling, dizzying world. He began punching and kicking at the thing in front of him and quite suddenly it shrunk. As it did so, he staggered past it and collapsed on the ground.

He lay there, exhausted. Once he turned to

Treetime

make sure that he was really outside the circle, then he stretched out again on the cool green grass. The world still spun, but more slowly now, lazily. He could feel that the merry-go-round was coming to a halt. When everything was quite still again, he got to his feet.

There was a movement not far away in the grass. When Alan turned to see what it was, it was another one of the toadstools and it was making its way round behind him. Beyond it, others were doing the same thing. The whole circle of toadstools was expanding, closing him in again.

With a cry he dashed for the gap that remained and this time he sprinted well away before stopping to look back. He was learning now about this place called Treetime. It was a dangerous, unreliable place and he could not afford to be careless. Of course, whatever could enchant a massive tree could also enchant a boy! From now on he would be on his guard. He was free and he would make sure that he stayed free.

The circle of toadstools had apparently given up on him and had returned to their previous positions. They looked small and harmless in the long grass. The one that Alan had punched hadn't moved but still lay in rubbery fragments.

He grinned as it dawned on him what this meant. What could be easier? he thought.

He trotted back to the toadstools and, one by one, just kicked them away, laughing happily. He even imagined they were small red and white footballs and that he was the penalty-taker.

'Goal!' he murmured to himself as each of the toadstools burst into small pieces.

Then, with a quick look round to make sure he hadn't missed any, he walked back up to the oak tree and hammered again on the trunk.

He was right. Nothing could have been easier. But if he had been as careful as he had promised that he would be, he might have asked himself why none of Oak's friends among the trees, not even Whispering Beech herself, had chosen to make such short work of Silver Birch's little army.

8 Broad Oak

Broad Oak woke slowly. Alan hammered and shouted, and at last he was rewarded by the sound of Oak's deep, rough voice.

'Who's knocking?' it said. 'Who's knocking and calling?'

It took the tree a few moments to come to its senses.

'Oh yes, I got a shock from Tricky Birch's sneaky crew. Ah, someone's kicked the caps off them. Capital.' Then he saw the boy. 'Who could you be?' he asked.

'Alan. My name's Alan. It was me who destroyed the toadstools.'

'Well, thanks. Kind of you. But what's a kid like you doing awake in Treetime? You should be back in your bunk.'

Alan liked the oak. You could trust him. He started to tell the story of how the ash had got hold of him, but the oak interrupted.

'Skip here quick and climb up,' he said. 'We must make tracks. There's work to do.'

Alan looked up at the great tree wondering whether he could climb it.

Treetime

'Come round the back of my trunk,' said the oak helpfully. 'There are cracks and knuckles and kinks at the back.'

There were. It still wasn't easy, but Alan managed to pull himself to the lowest branch.

'Climb further,' urged Broad Oak. 'Fork to fork, that's the trick.'

Actually, the climb got easier as the boy went up. Each time he stopped, the oak encouraged him to go a little higher.

'I've got a good thick fork near my peak,' he said. 'You can tuck in there.'

It was higher than Alan had ever climbed before, but he felt quite safe in Broad Oak's hundreds of arms and when he had got as far as he could go, there was a perfect place for him to sit, wedged between two branches.

'Look out and stick close, I'd like to get cracking,' the oak said.

Alan noticed that his voice did not come from far below, but from all around, from every twig and every leaf. And as Broad Oak picked up speed, the air rushed through the branches and a whole world of leaves fluttered and muttered and danced to and fro, and Alan felt like a woodland prince on a ride through a forest that had no end.

The oak didn't roll and hop like the ash, or

Broad Oak

glide like the beech or skate like the pines or scamper like Berry Elder. The oak cantered. Yes, kantered.

For Alan, it was the ride of his life.

'Now we can talk,' said the oak from every side. '*You* can talk. I shall call you Kirk.'

'But my name's Alan.'

'OK, but I like Kirk better. Or Rick, or Mick or Jack.'

'Jack, then.'

'OK. Jack.'

So Alan told him about Ash and the daddy-long-legs and the swing and about his battle with the toadstools.

'Lucky for me,' said the oak, 'but awkward for you, I reckon.'

'Why?'

'Because you must look out with Tricky Birch. A curious kind of tree is Sneaky Birch and she won't be keen on your kicking the caps off her wicked crew.'

'But I'm safe up here with you, aren't I?'

'Of course, but lurk quietly in my fork.'

'Where are we going? Can we go and see if my home is all right?'

'Beech will take care of the cottage. We have to make for the muck.'

'For the *muck*?'

53

Treetime

'The sticky, sunken neck of the woods. I don't much like the muck.'

Alan laughed.

'We call it the marsh,' he said.

'Yes, but muck's better. Thicker and stickier.'

'Do you like birds, Oak?'

'Yes, I like birds. Some kinds.'

'I bet you like rooks and ducks and storks.'

Broad Oak seemed surprised.

'That's very quick of you, Jack. I like rooks and ducks and storks and kestrels and larks. But how did you reckon that?'

'Just luck,' said Alan happily.

They sped on over the countryside. Alan peered out between the forest of leaves but it was hard to know where on earth they were. The big stretch of woodland that should have been in front of them had disappeared, and even the hedges had gone, leaving only a line of dead leaves and brambles and nettles to show where they had been.

'Why are we going to the muck, Oak?'

'To seek out Wicker Willow and a few other blokes who didn't make it to the Clock. The trees of the muck have no knack for talk, but we may need to pick some of them up if it comes to the crunch.'

But Oak was not the first of the big trees to have had this idea. As they began going down

Broad Oak

towards the marsh, they realized that the whole area was shrouded in a dense fog.

'Pluck-a-duck!' said the oak. 'A murk thick enough to sink us.'

'Can't you see in the fog?' asked Alan nervously.

'No.'

They had slowed right down and the fog was like a solid wall around them.

'This is one of Ash's tricks,' said Oak. 'He likes a murk, does bleak Mister Ash.'

'But surely trees can't make fog,' said Alan.

'Ash can,' said Oak. 'And he knows that I can't stick a murk, and nor can Beech or Sycamore or Cedar. This is to block the big folk.'

Oak moved cautiously forward and called out from time to time.

'Willow! It's Oak!'

Other trees loomed around them now, but there was no answering call.

'I'm trekking back,' said Oak, and he turned round and started up the slope again. But he couldn't see any more than Alan could, and instead of making his way up the gentle slope they had come down, he arrived at a high bank. A much higher bank than he realized.

'Cling on, Jack,' he called, and Alan felt him suddenly spring into the air in an effort to reach the top of the bank.

Treetime

But Oak was altogether too stout and heavy to be much good at springing. He landed less than half-way up the slope and there was no way that his bundled-up roots could hold on. The whole tree started to topple backwards.

Oak only just saved himself from falling full length on the ground. He teetered and lurched and somehow slid back down to the bottom of the bank where he managed to get back into an upright position.

'That was nearly a bad break, Jack,' he called out cheerfully.

But Alan wasn't there to hear him. When Broad Oak had first landed, the boy had simply been catapulted from his spot and found himself flying through the air on a journey that might easily have broken his neck. Would have done so, in fact, had it not been for the marsh itself.

9 The Murk

Instead of being flung on to hard ground, Alan landed with a splash in a metre or so of filthy water. He choked and spluttered, but it was only a pool and his flailing arms soon hit against a piece of ground firm enough for him to pull himself out of the water.

'Oak!' he called desperately, and began stumbling towards the place where he thought Oak had been. But immediately he fell into a boggy mire that sucked at his legs.

Then he heard Oak's voice.

'Alan! Alan!' it called. 'This way!'

He dragged himself through the swamp towards the sound. So Oak had come back for him! He felt proud to be Oak's friend.

The ground grew a little drier.

'Come on, Alan,' said the voice again.

The voice was muffled and rather strange, but then everything was strange in this blanket of mist.

The tree loomed in front of him and the boy began to run towards it. He was already under its branches when a little nagging feeling in the boy's mind – a little nagging feeling that was searching around for something that it knew wasn't quite right – suddenly found what it was after.

The boy stopped in his tracks.

'What's my name, Oak?' he shouted.

'Alan, of course. Come on, young Alan.'

Alan turned and fled. The lowest of the branches swept against his face as he ran.

Oak would have called him Jack. Not only was it not Oak, but Alan knew exactly who it was. At close range, there was no mistaking the moist and chilly tones of Mister Ash.

Alan ran and hopped and stumbled and tripped, and the third time he fell over he found himself under the branches of another tree. But who was it this time? Perhaps this was Silver Birch?

Yet something in him knew that it was not. The shadow above him was very dark and dense and the trunk in front of him was black as night. Rather than turn away again and risk running slap back into the arms of Mister Ash, the boy stayed where he was and called out cautiously.

'Who's there?' he said.

'It is I,' replied a deep, melancholy voice.

'And who are you?' Alan didn't much like the sound of this voice either.

'I'm Yew,' returned the voice.

'You're *me*? You're not me! Whoever you are, you're *not* me.'

The Murk

Alan was not afraid and he was getting angry. He was angry at this confusing, foggy world with tricky trees and quagmires.

'Not you. Yew,' said the tree sternly.

'Stop talking in riddles. I'm me. Who are you?'

'What a rude, bad-tempered boy it is! I am the yew tree, the church tree, the holy tree some would say.'

Alan remembered and laughed. There were several large yew trees in the churchyard. Their berries were poisonous, his mother had told him. And there was a smell about them, a smell of something old and musty.

'And whose side are you on?' asked the boy.

'I'm on nobody's side. I'm on the side of right and truth.'

That sounded all right, but Alan didn't like the way it was said.

'You mean you're with Oak and Beech?' he asked.

'I told you. I'm not with anybody. I have my own work to do.'

'Can you see in the fog?'

'Of course. All ways are lit by the inner light.'

'Can you please help me to get out of here?'

'I will help all who turn to me if their hearts are pure.'

Alan thought about this. His heart had never

seemed very pure to him, but perhaps no one else would know this.

'That's OK then,' he said. 'Can I climb up?'

'Climb up? Certainly not. You stay where you are. Not that you'd be able to climb up anyway, for the way of truth is a hard and bristly way.'

'But how can you help me if you won't let me up?'

'I didn't in fact say that I would help you. I told you that I had my own work to do. Treetime is an important time for a holy yew. I must visit all of my fellow-trees and offer them succour.'

'*Sucker?*'

'Yes, succour. Help, advice, guidance. That is my task.'

'But that's exactly what I need.'

The yew pondered a moment.

'But you're not a tree.'

'What difference does that make? You only said: anyone with a pure heart.'

'Any tree with a pure heart, I meant.'

'Has Oak got a pure heart?'

'No. Too coarse and bold.'

'Beech?'

'No. Too lofty and proud.'

'Ash?'

'No. Ash is cunning and jealous.'

'What about Silver Birch?'

The Murk

'Good lord, no. Weird and superstitious. My word no. Birch indeed!'

'Who, then?'

'Well, there's Hazel, I suppose. She's rather sweet, though too vain, of course. And Cedar's all right but very selfish. Some of the smaller trees are harmless enough, but they've all got their faults. They all need to be shown the true way.'

'It sounds as if the holy yews are the only pure ones.'

'Exactly. Quite right. I'm glad you recognize it.'

'But that means that you can only help yourselves.'

'Wrong. Very wrong. A yew must help all those who need help and none need help more than the wicked.'

'If I told you I was wicked, would you help me? I mean, there's no one else around to help, is there?'

It was obvious to Alan that Holy Yew liked fine words better than good deeds and he saw that he was only going to get help if he could somehow trick Yew into it.

'So you're a wicked little boy, are you?'

'Yes.'

'Then I can only help you if you promise never to be wicked again.'

'I promise.'

Treetime

It seemed an easy enough promise to make, simply because it was clearly impossible to keep.

'Very well then.'

'Shall I climb up?'

'You shall not. You shall come close to my trunk and walk alongside me. You shall not touch me and you shall only speak when you're spoken to.'

'If you'll just see me out of the fog, to somewhere I know where I am . . .'

'I shall decide how you should be helped. And you shall remain silent. I must not be disturbed while I carry out my work. Let us proceed.'

The fog was still thick and it was impossible to tell where they were heading. Holy Yew went slowly, but seemed to have no trouble seeing where he was going.

'The fog's getting thicker,' said Alan.

'Be quiet.'

'Please, Holy Yew, I want to get *home*,' said the boy after what seemed like an endless time tramping blindly along next to his stern guide.

'Home! You have no idea of where you want to go. Home is just a word. You think home is a house with a family and a warm bed, but do you know, I ask myself, where is the home of the spirit? Do you know the way to *that* home?'

'Perhaps not, but . . .'

The Murk

'Be silent I said.'

The home of the spirit sounded rather unpleasant, like a haunted castle. Alan wondered whether it was time to leave the company of Holy Yew, but he took one look at the fog that pressed closely around them and decided that it wasn't. At least they were going somewhere, and at least he was safe for the time being from Mister Ash.

'Here we are,' said Yew, stopping.

'Where?'

The fog, if anything, was thicker than ever.

'We may say goodbye now, and you may thank me.'

'Thank you for *what*? You haven't done anything for me.'

The yew laughed drily.

'Oh, but I have,' he said. 'I have brought you to the very centre of the fog. This is where you must start. From the darkest, most difficult spot of all. That is the way, you see, although you'd need to be a lot older and wiser to understand the reason why. The wicked cannot expect to lose their wickedness just like that, you know. They must be right at the middle of the most difficult part before they can start their journey towards the light. Only thus can they hope to be saved. Goodbye then.'

Treetime

'But hold on! Where am I? Tell me that at least.'

'How can I tell you where you are when you don't even know where you want to go?' said the yew obscurely.

And with surprising swiftness, he spun round and disappeared into the fog.

10 Lonely Alder

Utterly lost and totally alone, Alan stood and shivered in the fog.

After a while he realized that there was a noise in his ears. A swishing, swirling, rolling, rumbling sort of noise that appeared to be coming from everywhere at once and getting louder and softer in turns.

It seemed to the boy as if whatever was making the noise was gathering somewhere far off and then rushing towards him and sweeping past him, and gathering itself again. What on earth was this place that the holy yew had brought him to?

Then suddenly he knew that what he was hearing was the sound of the river, and the river was in a tremendous hurry and very close at hand.

Yet he still couldn't make out just where it was. It was as if the sound of the water had got tied up with the fog and was whirling all around him. It even seemed to him that he was on a small island right in the middle of the river and that if he took a single step in any direction he would find himself plunged into the current. So he stood stock-still and yelled.

'Help!'

'What's that?' said a voice behind him. 'Did somebody say something?'

Alan spun round to see who had spoken, but could see nothing.

'Who's there?' he said nervously.

'Why, can't you see me?' said the voice. It was a deep, pleasant, lazy sort of voice. A reedy, relaxing sort of voice.

'I can't see a thing,' said Alan. 'I'm in the middle of the river and I can't see anything but fog. Where are you?'

'Here where I always am,' the voice replied. 'And you're not in the middle of the river. The river's just over *there* and I'm just over *here*.'

'Are you a tree?'

There was a woody chuckle.

'Am I a tree? Put it this way. I'm as much a tree as you are a boy and the river's a river and the fog is fog.'

'Can I come closer to you? Without falling in, I mean.'

'Come as close as you like. You seem to be in some kind of trouble, although I can't think why. It's all quite simple and friendly. The river won't eat you, the fog won't eat you and I certainly won't eat you. But I must say that it's an odd day to choose for fishing.'

Lonely Alder

Alan took a few careful steps towards where the voice was coming from.

'I didn't come for fishing!' he said. 'It's Treetime and I want to go home, but I can't because I'm lost in the fog.'

'Oh yes. Treetime,' said the tree without enthusiasm. 'A pointless sort of business if you ask me. I thought you were just another boy come to fish. That's the only kind of boy I ever see down here. Sometimes they get their lines caught up in me and sometimes they leave them caught up in me and I wish they wouldn't. But on the whole I've got nothing against them. They seem to like the river in their way. But you are not here to fish. And you want to go home, and you can't see in the fog. But really, there's no problem. The fog will go away sooner or later as it always does. Stay here for a while and then go home later.'

'But the fog might go on for ages.'

'It might, but probably it won't. It'll no doubt go away at the end of Treetime, if not before.'

'The end of Treetime! Could it last as long as that?'

'How long *is* that?'

There was no sensible answer to this question. Time had stopped. Only the trees were moving. And him. And the river.

'Well, it can't be for ever, I suppose,' he said

thoughtfully, 'because the river's still moving. And that means that time hasn't completely stopped. It must only *seem* to have stopped.'

'That's a very clever thought, young man,' said the tree, who sounded interested for the first time. 'Even a river doesn't last for ever. Even this wonderful, life-giving, ever-changing river won't last for ever. But not many people would have thought of that. Only trees like me that stay in one place and watch and think. I'm impressed. What's your name?'

'Alan. Or . . . or Jack if you like.'

'Two names! Goodness me. That sounds very extravagant. Well, of course I prefer Alan. Jack's a bit dry and hard. Not much *water* in it, if you see what I mean. But Alan is a good, liquid kind of name. Not unlike my own name, in fact.'

'You can see in the fog, can't you? Will you take me home please?'

'Oh that's quite impossible, I'm afraid. I *never* move,' said the tree.

'Not even in Treetime?'

'That's rather a silly question. I'm less impressed. Since trees *only* move in Treetime, you can't say *even* in Treetime, can you?'

Alan got confused.

'I'm sure you're right, but can't you please move just this once and take me home?'

Lonely Alder

'Do you know who I am?'

Alan moved right up to the tree and peered upwards to where the branches and leaves disappeared into the fog.

'No, I don't know who you are. I can't see much of you anyway.'

'I'm Alder. Lonely Alder, they call me. When they talk about me at all. Which, I'm sure, is not often. Anyway, I don't care for the word lonely. It sounds as if I might not like being on my own.'

'Are all alders on their own?'

'I've no idea. Since I don't move around, I know nothing of what the others do or don't do, and I don't care. Do all boys go fishing?'

'No, not all.'

'But some like it very much?'

'Yes.'

'There you are, you see. It's the same. Not all alders are alone but some like it very much.'

'I would have thought you'd like to move around in Treetime.'

'Why?'

'To see another view, another part of the river.'

'I don't want another view and I'm perfectly happy with this part of the river. I know it and it knows me. It gives me everything I need and in return I give it . . .' The alder lapsed into silence.

'What do you give it?' urged the boy.

Treetime

'I give it my love,' said the alder very quietly. But he obviously didn't like to talk of such things and he went on in a different tone. 'I like everything about it here and I cannot imagine liking it nearly as much anywhere else. I like the pools and the shallows and the eddies and the backwaters. I like it when the river's high and fast and when it's low and slow. I like it when it's a trickle. I like it when it's a flood. I like the dragonflies and the kingfishers and the lazy chub and the bright dace. I'm not very fond of canoes. Now, since you're here and obviously don't want to stay here as I do, give me one good reason why I should go to the trouble of hauling up my roots and setting off over foreign fields and dry soil.'

'You see, Old Elm is dead,' the boy began.

'Bad luck,' said Alder.

Then Alan told him about Oak and Birch and Ash and the angry thorns.

'Big-tree politics,' was Alder's comment.

'But my home's going to be destroyed.'

'Find another home. A better one, nearer the river.'

'But don't you see,' said the boy desperately, 'that's just it. My home for me is what this place is to you. It's the place I like best. I like my room and my things and the meals and the garden and the walks and the swing. I just . . . I just love it.'

Lonely Alder

Alder went silent.

'I do see that. Yes, I can understand that. Brick walls and a garden are nothing compared to a river, certainly, but I see what you mean.'

'Just think if someone was going to destroy your river.'

'Nobody could do that.'

'Yes they could. They could poison it or dam it or make it go somewhere else.'

'If anybody dared to do that I'd . . . I'd . . .'

'You'd fight for it, wouldn't you? In Treetime at least.'

'I would.'

'But that's what I want to do. Please help me, Lonely Alder.'

There was another long silence.

'Very well. I will. But I will not leave the river. I might never find it again. What I will do for you is unearth myself and fall into the stream. You can jump on top of me and we'll float along together until we get out of the fog. Then you're on your own.'

Alan could see a flaw in this plan but he didn't at first want to mention it. Yet Alder was doing him a great favour and it seemed unfair not to be honest.

'How will you get back again, Alder?'

Alder laughed.

'I don't suppose I'd be much good at walking,' he said, 'never having tried it. But I guess I could paddle myself slowly back upriver, keeping out of the current. I've got plenty of paddles.'

So it was arranged. Alan had to stand back while the alder shook himself and wobbled a bit and loosened his roots, and there was a sucking noise just underground, followed by a series of squelches as the great rootweb freed itself from the soggy soil.

Then, rather abruptly and without any warning, Alder fell forward into the river.

'Jump!' sang out a gurgly voice.

Alan jumped, and a moment later was hauling himself aboard the floating alder.

He was wet again, and plastered with mud from head to toe, and his tracksuit was torn in a dozen places, but it was a fine trip downstream astride Alder's trunk.

Nobody could have called their progress rapid. They swung to and fro in the current, now colliding with one bank and now with the other, and all sorts of flotsam got caught up in Alder's roots and branches. A plank floated by them and Alan grabbed it up and used it to fend themselves clear of the banks.

Alder was enjoying himself.

'So this is what it's like to go swimming,' he said.

Lonely Alder

His voice was still gurgly, and indeed nearly all of him was beneath the surface of the water, but he didn't seem to mind.

'River below, river ahead, river behind and river on both sides,' he said contentedly.

'But you told me you don't like canoes,' the boy said, laughing.

'I might change my mind,' was Alder's reply.

'Are you on your back or your front?' Alan asked.

'Neither and both,' said the alder. 'I don't have a back and front.'

'But are you looking up or down? How do you see, anyway? Have you got eyes?'

He'd wondered about that before when he was travelling with Broad Oak, but had forgotten to ask.

'Plenty of them,' said the alder. 'I must have twenty or thirty and I'm not even very big as trees go.'

'You mean all those little knots and seams?'

'That's what we see through,' said Alder.

Alan tried to imagine what it was like to see through twenty eyes. It made him dizzy to think about it.

'The fog's clearing,' said Alder.

Alan looked up from his paddling to see the blanket of fog unthreading around them. Thin

Lonely Alder

patches of it drifted here and there above the river, getting thinner.

Ahead of them loomed a more solid shape.

'Look out, Alder! It's the bridge ahead!'

But the bridge wasn't the problem. The problem was the weir underneath it, where the river suddenly funnelled and rushed and which was no place for a canoe, let alone for a full-grown alder with a passenger.

'There's a weir, Alder! Get to the bank!'

But Alder heard only the rushing of the water as it gathered speed towards the bridge and Alder didn't know what a weir was. He slid happily into the hastening current.

'So this is canoeing!' he cried.

Well, it was, in a way. But Alder didn't know what no canoeist should forget. To check the depth of white water.

Under the middle of the bridge, he stuck. It was not a temporary check, it was a total, irreversible, grinding halt. It was the end of Alder's first trip.

Alan knew where he was now. He didn't like to leave his new friend in such a fix, but he was desperate to get home.

'You run off,' Alder gurgled. 'Don't worry about me. I'll find a way out.'

Already his branches were pushing and paddling against the stream.

Treetime

'Are you sure?' asked the boy.

'Don't you worry about me, I said. The old river and I have been friends too long for us not to find a way of settling this. I'll get home all right. You'd better hurry off and see about your little matter.'

One of Alder's larger branches had caught against the arch of the bridge and Alan climbed up it and on to the road.

'Goodbye, Alder. Thank you,' he called down.

'Goodbye. And good luck,' said Alder. 'No need for thanks. This is a trip I wouldn't have missed. I shall appreciate the river even more after this. I never knew quite how lively and . . . *powerful* it is. And don't forget to come and visit me at my place one day.'

11 Tricky Birch

Alan set off for home. The fog had gone and he knew the way, but the countryside still looked very strange without even a copse or a thicket to be seen. There were a few trees on the move here and there, apparently travelling in the same direction as he was.

He began trotting to get warm, and then running as fast as he could as he thought of what might be happening to his home.

So it happened that he was almost out of breath and his eyes were fixed on the ground in front of him when he came to the top of a small hill. There were high banks on either side of the road. And it was here that he met the toadstools.

They were densely packed across the road, and more of them suddenly appeared on the banks to left and right.

Alan spun round. Toadstools and mushrooms of every kind were hurrying down the banks behind him. Legions of them. He was surrounded.

There was no talking in the toadstool army, and no commands. But they all knew just what to do. They closed in on all sides, and then they began getting bigger.

Oh *no*! thought the boy.

This time the spell was immediate. There was no dizziness, no merry-go-round, no chance of escape. All at once Alan found himself on what seemed to be some kind of cloud and all around him there were faces. Some were very long and droopy and some were almost quite round and some of them were deep red and some bright red and some pinkish and some brownish and some were completely white, and all of them had hats or hoods or cowls and it was impossible to say where the hats or hoods or cowls ended and the faces began.

It felt like a cloud that he was sitting on, kind of puffy and uncertain, but it actually worked more like a waterbed, squashing down in one place and plumping up in another whenever he moved.

The world had gone out of shape, too. It wasn't flat any more. There were no horizons. The ranks of faces climbed up and all around and when Alan looked above him, instead of the sky he saw a great dome with gills and it seemed that he was inside a giant mushroom with mushroom-face walls and a toadstool-cap sky, and for some reason the whole thing seemed extraordinarily funny and he lay back and laughed.

But what a laugh!

Could it really be his, this rubbery, spongy, burbling chorus of sound?

He laughed again, and again a great quivering pool of laughter wallowed around him, and then he realized that all the faces were laughing too, even the long and droopy ones and that the whole giant mushroom world was simmering in one huge laugh.

Then one of the faces close to him spoke.

'He's got a good laugh!' it said. And 'good laugh, good laugh, laugh, laugh, laugh' went the chorus.

Alan laughed again and bounced up and down a few times on his puff-ball bed. And the more he laughed, the more the faces laughed, and Alan knew what it was like to be in a balloon of laughter.

Then suddenly he found that everything around him had gone still and that he was the only one laughing, and he felt rather stupid, giggling to himself.

Another face bulged forward beside him.

'Goal!' it reminded him.

'Goal, goal, goal!' came the chorus.

But the sound was lugubrious now, like a long groan.

Alan remembered. 'Goal!' he had said as he had kicked the little red-and-white toadstools.

Tricky Birch

And he remembered why he had been ambushed and why he was here.

Nobody was laughing now. Alan, in fact, was crying silently.

'That's right, goal-kicker, blub,' said another face. 'Blub, blub, blub.'

'Where am I?' said Alan feebly.

'Mushroom Cloud Nine,' came the reply.

'Nine, nine, nine,' the chorus sang.

And Alan cried, because he didn't know how to make this brimming, shifting, rubbery world go away. And all at once the faces began swelling and gushing, and Alan saw that there were tears running down the faces, the droopy ones and the round ones, and they all merged together as they swelled, and either they went up or the great toadstool cap came down for Alan found himself sitting on the ground, and there was something at his back.

It was a tree trunk, and when Alan turned round, he saw that it was a pale silver, peeling here and there like delicate paper. It belonged to Silver Birch.

Then he heard her sing-song voice above him.

'It's hard to tell, hard to tell
How he made his escape from the mushroom spell,

> *But little did he think that I'M HERE AS WELL.'*

Alan began edging very slowly away from Silver Birch's trunk. They were beside the road, not far from where he'd been ambushed. Very carefully he started drawing his feet up under him, getting ready to run.

> *'There's no point at all in running away,'*

sang Silver Birch merrily,

> *'For I'm quick as the time 'twixt the night and the day.*
> *No point at all, no point at all,*
> *For I'm the quickest of all.'*

Suddenly she slipped away from behind him and sprang nimbly to the other side of the road and back, to stand over him once more.

> *'I've come and I've gone to the edge of the track,*
> *With a hop and a skip I've been and I'm back.*
> *I know the earth and I use the breeze,*
> *None can outpace me with friends like these.*
> *I've gone and I'm back, I've come and I've been,*
> *So stay where you are if you see what I mean.'*

Tricky Birch

Alan saw very well what she meant. She would have caught him before he had even started.

She didn't seem cruel like Ash, or unpleasant like the holy yew, but Oak had called her tricky. 'Look out for Tricky Birch,' he'd said.

Alan decided to see if he could get anywhere by being friendly.

'How did I escape from the mushroom world, though, Silver Birch? I mean, what was the secret?' he asked in his politest little-boy voice.

> *'No reason not to tell the boy,*
> *Who only wants to be friends.*
> *The secret is that the crying must start*
> *As soon as the laughter ends.'*

Alan couldn't quite make this out, but he did notice that it hadn't taken Silver Birch long to spot his little plan. She was certainly a lot cleverer than Holy Yew. Or Broad Oak, for that matter.

> *'Find the road between laughter and tears*
> *And the mushroom world just disappears,'*

sang Silver Birch.

> *'You really are a lucky lad*
> *To find it so funny and then so sad.'*

Alan didn't feel lucky. He knew that his home was only just beyond the hill now, but it might just as well have been miles away. Silver Birch was too fast for him and too clever as well, and she didn't seem to be in a hurry to go anywhere.

'I can't run away from you, but I want to go home. Can't we go home together, please, Silver Birch?' he said.

'But that would never never do
What with me being me and you being you
For as long as I'm here and I've got you too,
Then Ash and the thorns will do what they'll do.
But if I take you back to see what we'll see
There's Oak and there's Beech to set you free
And freedom for you and freedom for me
Are two different things as they'll always be
For your freedom's for you and mine is for TREE!'

The birch laughed happily and did a little dance round the boy where he sat. But as she did so, he had a thought. It wasn't a very difficult thought and maybe he should have had it before. But it was only when Silver Birch was dancing around him that he noticed her shape. None of her branches were close to the ground, and they all pointed upwards. And all of them were rather on the short side.

She could outrun him all right, but he couldn't

Tricky Birch

see how on earth she was going to stop him or pick him up.

He didn't give himself time to think any more. He got up and fled.

Silver Birch was there beside him instantly, springing effortlessly along. Then she darted suddenly in front of him and he had to swerve to miss her. Then again she was in front, but he sidestepped her again. And the next time he sold her a dummy that they would have been proud of him for on the football field, and it sent her the wrong way. Still she sprang after him, heading him off, but they were over the rise now and there before them was the little valley where his house stood.

He almost stopped dead in his astonishment. It wasn't the little valley he knew, with its few meadows and fences and hedges, it was a dense forest.

Every tree from the whole area must have been there. And somewhere right in the middle of them all was a small cottage. If the small cottage still stood.

Alan dashed on down the slope.

Silver Birch could have run circles round him. But the boy had been right. There was no way for her to grab him, and she was getting cross.

Once she barged right into him and nearly

Treetime

knocked him flying. Twice she tried to trip him up with her roots. But it was not for nothing that Alan was known as the best under-11 striker in the school. He dummied and he swerved and he leapt and he ran, and quite suddenly found himself running into a forest that had not been there the night before.

12 The Fourteen Tribes

The trees were standing closely together and there were hundreds of them. It was dark among their trunks and the sky was quite blotted out.

As he ran into the forest, Alan took a look over his shoulder and glimpsed something silvery slipping among the trees behind him, but he knew that it was impossible for the birch to follow him here. And there didn't seem much danger of being grabbed by Mister Ash, either. It was very dark and he was very small among the tall trees.

Besides, the trees seemed busy with their own concerns. Many of them were still on the move, making their way to other parts of the wood, and there was a good deal of jostling and plenty of tangling of branches and twigs.

A small tree rushed by on a great bundle of roots and Alan was caught up and swept along for a few metres. Next he was nearly squashed between two slender trees that went for the same narrow gap.

Then he found himself among the willows, and here he was spotted. There were bog willows and marsh willows and wickers and withies and

weepers. They clustered thickly around him and he dodged this way and that trying to find a way between them. But some of them had trunks that lay almost flat before curling upwards, and others grew in loops and twists and spirals, and many of them had branches that reached all the way to the ground, and all of them were trying to trip him up and circle him round and lead him wherever they would.

Then all at once the trees were still, apparently listening to something, and for a moment there was a complete quiet as every living tree stood mortal still.

Alan, too, stopped, wondering what the trees had heard. As he looked up he saw that the tops of the trees around him had started to stir in a slight breeze. At first it was no more than the faintest breath of wind, but as the boy watched, it grew stronger and a murmur ran through the treetops and Alan thought that there was an anxiety in it as if the breeze had brought bad news.

Suddenly it dawned on him what the bad news was. The wind was awake again and it meant that Treetime was coming to an end. It was coming to an end!

And at the same moment that Alan had this thought, he saw that there was a pathway open before him, and right at the end of it he could see the little cottage that was his home.

There were trees ranged to the right and left of the path. On Alan's right were the willows who had been teasing him. On his left was a throng of little elders that all looked exactly like the berry elder who had got so excited at the First Clock. Alan trotted down the path between them, and he could feel some of the trees looking at him, but none of them moved from their spots. It seemed that they were waiting for something to happen.

He could see the cottage clearly now and began to quicken his pace. He cared for nothing but to get inside his home. He didn't even want to look for Broad Oak. He just wanted to run to the kitchen door, open it, get inside and slam the door behind him. And bolt it.

But it wasn't to be quite as simple as that. A small band of trees appeared at the end of the path, between the boy and the house. They were young saplings, slender and swift, and Alan saw them position themselves in front of the cottage. He could tell by their leaves that they were ashes, and they were waiting for him.

There were lots of things that Alan could have done if he had taken time to think. He could have dived in among the elders and hidden himself until he got a chance to find out where Broad Oak was. He could have disappeared anywhere inside

The Fourteen Tribes

the forest and worked his way carefully round to the other side of the cottage.

But his home was too close. He could even see the yellow of the back door. So he did the first thing that came into his head and made a dash for the house.

The ash saplings laughed and drew closer together. He was making it so easy for them! Their laughter was like old Mister Ash's, chilly and moist.

Alan put on his best burst of speed and tried to run round them, but they laughed again and moved to head him off. Finally, because there was nothing else for it, he turned and ran straight at them.

They laughed again, louder, and closed ranks. Alan put his head down, closed his eyes and dived towards one of the narrow gaps. But at the last moment he felt a tug from behind him, he felt twigs clutch his clothes, he felt shoots reach round his body and he felt himself suddenly lifted right off the ground. Lifted and lifted, high in the air. Out of reach of the ashes, higher than the house itself.

It was Whispering Beech who had saved him. Just as the laughing Ashes were stretching out their branches to grab him, Whispering Beech had glided quickly forward from where she stood

Treetime

at the head of the beeches, bowed low like a tall courtier before the throne, reached out her longest and most supple branch and swept the boy off his feet and high into the air.

He had a brief vision of fluttering leaves, of a sea of treetops, before he felt himself lowered swiftly down towards the roof of his house. At the same time he heard Beech's rustling whisper from behind him. 'Good fortune be on your house,' it sang.

The shoots and twigs that held the boy began to loosen their hold and for a moment he thought he would fall. Then he saw, right in front of him, the window of the attic where Mister Ash had grabbed him the night before. He reached out, seized hold of the window frame and pulled himself into the room.

How strange to find his room just as he had left it! So much had happened and yet here everything was the same. His bedclothes were flung back where he'd jumped out of bed to close the window. Glass still littered the floor.

He pulled on a pair of trainers so his feet wouldn't get cut and raced down the stairs and slipped first into his mum's room and then into Emily's. They were both sleeping soundly. As he stood by his mum's bed he wanted to reach out and wake her, but something in him knew for certain that she would not wake, and warned him not to try.

Once in the attic again he looked out of each of the four windows in turn. The trees were still motionless, but they were not, as he had thought, standing around haphazardly. The path he had run up between the elders and the willows was one of a dozen such paths, all running in straight lines directly towards the cottage. The trees stood in neat sections, like the slices of a cake.

Of course! It was the Great Clock. And that was exactly what it looked like from the attic windows: a great clock of trees, with the little cottage at the very centre. The trees were all standing with their own kind. He could see the ashes, with Mister Ash himself at their head, and he felt a leap of joy in his heart when he saw the massive shape of Broad Oak with all the other oaks standing behind him.

The trouble was that he could hear nothing of what was going on outside. He wondered if he should have stayed among the trees. Now he had no idea what was being said. And even if he shouted at the top of his voice, no one would hear him either.

At the last of the four windows he heard a whirring sound close to his ear. He spun round with a wild hope.

Treetime

A daddy-long-legs flew by and settled on the windowsill.

'Daddy-long-legs!' cried the boy. 'Is that you?'

'Certainly it's me,' replied the thin, metallic voice. 'How many are there of us spinning around in Treetime, do you think? Anyway, I'm here because I was looking for you.'

'Were you really?'

'After you got away from Ash, I stayed where I was. As you know, we're better at listening than at moving around. So I stayed in Ash's hollow and kept a few ears open for his plans. I was there when he nearly got you at the marsh. I tried to warn you but you couldn't hear me, of course. I sent out messages on every frequency known to bugs but I'm afraid your listening equipment is rather . . . *clumsy*, shall we say. If you'd been a daddy-long-legs you'd have been blown away screaming with your legs over your ears. As it is you heard nothing. Still, you seemed to do all right without me. How did you know it wasn't Oak, by the way?'

'His voice wasn't right, there weren't enough K sounds and he didn't know Oak's special name for me. Hey, Daddy-long-legs, what's going on outside? I can't hear a thing.'

'It's OK. Nothing much is happening yet. The different groups are talking among themselves,

The Fourteen Tribes

deciding how to vote. I'm listening in, of course. In fact it's lucky for you that I'm here. It seems that they don't shout at each other at big meetings like this. They talk quietly and the words are carried from branch to branch and leaf to leaf.'

'But that must take ages.'

'It doesn't. They're very good at it. It's as if a wind blew through them carrying messages.'

'So it's going to be a vote, not a battle.' Alan wasn't sure if he was pleased about this. If it had been a battle, surely the huge oaks and the beeches would have made mincemeat of the ashes and thorns.

'Yes, it's going to be a vote. The striking of the Great Clock, they call it.'

'And what are they going to vote on?' asked Alan quietly.

The daddy-long-legs was silent for a moment.

'It's not really about your house. It's about whether people should be punished for the way they treat trees. A lot of the trees think that it's time people were taught a lesson. All the little hedge trees – the thorns and so on – are complaining about the way they get hacked and torn by the hedge-trimmers. The pines and spruces and larches say that they're never left to grow to full size, and what they hate worst is the way men plant them in rows. As if they were cabbages,

95

they said. Some of the others are angry about the poisoning of the waters they drink and the air they breathe.'

'What happens if the Clock votes against us?' Alan asked.

'It won't. It's only the ashes and thorns that really want to pull down your house.'

So that was it. Alan had a sudden vision of the house and everything in it strewn around the garden.

'But what about Mum, and Emily?'

'I told you. The Clock won't vote for it.'

Alan began counting on his fingers.

'Ashes, one. Thorns, two. Pines, you said, three. Birches, four. Yews, five. Willows, six. That's six already,' Alan said hopelessly.

The daddy-long-legs asked how he knew about the yews and willows, and Alan told him.

'So, you see, that's six out of twelve already,' said the boy.

'Six out of fourteen actually.'

'Fourteen? I thought they called it a clock.'

'Is there any good reason why a clock should only have twelve places?'

Alan considered the matter.

'Because there are twenty-four hours in a day,' he said, pleased with himself for thinking of something that the daddy-long-legs hadn't.

The Fourteen Tribes

'And how many hours in a Treetime?' It was a good question. Alan had little idea whether it had been hours or days since he had been grabbed from his attic room.

'Anyway, fourteen's their number,' went on the daddy-long-legs. 'The fourteen tribes of tree, Beech called them.'

'Come on to my shoulder, will you, Daddy – you don't mind me calling you Daddy, do you? – let's go and see who else is out there.'

The daddy-long-legs whirred up from the window and made rather a business of landing on Alan's shoulder.

'That's not my shoulder, that's my neck.'

'Sorry.'

The insect climbed down on to the boy's shoulder and they moved to the opposite window. The ashes were there in front of them with the thorns on their left. Mister Ash was closest to the house with the swing still dangling from its one remaining rope.

There were hundreds of thorns. Hawthorns, blackthorns, whitethorns, buckthorns and briars. They couldn't keep still, but kept jostling and barging and arguing.

Next to the thorns were the holy yews with some slender dark-green cypresses standing behind them pointing to the sky. And after them

Treetime

some trees that Alan didn't recognize.

'Who are that lot, Daddy?' he asked.

'Don't forget that I can't see like you can. I can't even tell if it's trees or a city out there. I have to listen to find out what's going on.'

'Aren't you listening now?'

'There are fourteen lots of trees out there! Even I can't listen to them all at once. What I'm doing is keeping a channel tuned to each of the groups and listening in to them in turn.'

'You're amazing, Daddy! You're a radio!'

'Can a radio talk? Can a radio think? Can a radio fly?' said the daddy-long-legs, insulted. 'The trouble with you humans is that you think you're the only clever ones. You telling me that I'm a radio is like me telling you that you're a robot and intending it as a compliment.'

'I'm sorry. I know you're clever, it's just that I didn't realize that something so small and sort of weak . . .'

'Fragile is the word you're looking for.'

'Yes. I didn't realize that something so small and fragile could do so many things.'

'To each his own,' said the daddy-long-legs. 'That tribe you don't recognize must be the limes and beams, by the way.'

They really didn't know how the limes and beams would vote, but Alan liked the sound of

The Fourteen Tribes

their names, so they counted them as friends.

The view from the next window was better. The first lot were the fruit trees, standing together like the most marvellous orchard you could imagine. Apples brushed shoulders with pears, and apricots with plums and peaches with cherries.

'They'll vote for us, I expect,' said Alan.

'I don't see why they should, to be honest,' said the daddy-long-legs.

'Because men plant them and water them and look after them.'

'I hope you're right.'

Next were the lofty beeches, allies for sure. After them came the sycamores, and Alan remembered how the sycamore at the Toot had always agreed with whatever had just been said.

'Good,' he said. 'They'll vote after Whispering Beech.'

Then there were the nut trees. Alan loved nuts – hazel nuts and almonds and walnuts – and couldn't believe that they would vote the wrong way. And the daddy-long-legs said that he had heard the sweet chestnuts and hazels talking earlier on and saying that they didn't get cut about nearly as much as they used to.

The first group to be seen at the next window were the pines. At their head was an enormous

Treetime

tree that towered above all the rest.

'Who on earth is that?' said Alan.

'That must be the one they call Big Red. He's an American redwood, the only one in these parts. "You'd better hope that Big Red doesn't get angry," I heard them saying to Oak.'

After the pines came the willows, and behind them, in the same slice of the clock, was a group of tall trees that Alan knew for poplars.

'Willows and poplars together,' he said. 'The willows don't like me, and I don't expect the poplars do either. They always seem so far away, even when you're right underneath them.'

The elders were next, and Alan was sure that Berry Elder would vote with Oak and Beech, and first in line at the next window were the oaks, who really needed more space and were standing with their great spreading branches entwined with those of their neighbours.

Right next to them was a small group of young trees who looked rather sad somehow, as if wondering where the rest of their tribe had got to. They were very few of them, no more than five or six, and none of them had grown very tall. Alan described them to the daddy-long-legs.

'Oh, they must be the young elms that Ash found and brought here,' said the little voice by the boy's ear.

The Fourteen Tribes

So that was why they looked sad. Nor was there much doubt about how *they* would vote.

Last of all were the silver birches. And there wasn't much doubt about them either.

Alan turned his head so that he could see his friend sitting on his shoulder.

'What's the score, then, Daddy?' he asked anxiously.

'If everybody votes as we think they will, the vote will be seven for us and seven against us,' the daddy-long-legs replied cheerfully. It seemed that he was good at mathematics as well. 'And that means they'll all go back to where they came from. The Big Sleep will start again and everything will be all right.'

'How come you know so much about everything, Daddy?'

'Because I've been listening to nothing but tree talk ever since this business started, and once I've heard something I remember it.'

Alan thought how useful it would be to have the daddy-long-legs on his shoulder when he was at school.

'When all this is over,' he said, 'will you live here in the attic with me? And come to school with me?'

'Hold on,' said the daddy-long-legs. 'The Great Clock's about to strike.' He was silent for a

Treetime

moment, apparently listening. 'Yes. Now we'll find out what's in store for us. Broad Oak is calling them to order.'

13 Bugging

'I'm going to try something quite difficult,' said the daddy-long-legs' dry and distant little voice from Alan's shoulder. 'As a matter of fact I'm not sure if it can be done, but I don't see why not. I'm going to set all my channels to receive and transmit at the same time. You should be able to hear what's going on outside without me saying anything. In fact I won't be *able* to say anything.'

'I'll hear the trees' own voices, you mean?'

'Yes. Just as if I was *only* a radio. If it works. Now this is a bit complicated so I'll go quiet now and you won't be able to talk to me until it's all over. Good luck.'

'But why can't you talk as well? I don't want you not to be here.'

There was no reply to this, only a humming noise which grew louder and then softer again.

Alan could just see the daddy-long-legs out of the corner of his eye. He watched as each part of the insect stirred and vibrated in turn. What a strange and wonderful little body it was!

'Can you hear me?' said Alan.

He didn't like the feeling of being alone. But

there was still no reply.

The daddy-long-legs sprang briefly in the air, landed, and the humming stopped. There was a silence and then a very faint voice could be heard, and it was not the voice of the daddy-long-legs.

'The Great Clock will strike,' it said. 'No heckling, no mocking, no mucking about.'

Alan bent his head closer to his shoulder to hear better, but he knew well enough whose voice he was listening to.

'Mister Ash will ask the question,' said Broad Oak. 'Then each kind of tree will make its remarks and cast its vote.'

'This is a simple matter, a sad matter, a straightforward matter,' came the sinister tones of Mister Ash. 'Shall we now punish the race of human beings for the death of Old Friend Elm . . .?'

There was a series of crackling sounds for a moment and Alan lost the next words. When the sound came back it was suddenly loud and clear and Alan jerked his ear away from his shoulder. The daddy-long-legs had apparently turned up the volume.

'The ash trees are of one mind,' said Mister Ash. 'We vote *yes*!'

Alan had moved to the east window to watch Ash while he spoke. The thorns were next.

'Clock strikes two,' called Oak.

'We proud thorns . . .' began one voice.

'Are of one mind . . .' went on another.

'And we vote . . .' said the third.

'Most definitely . . .' continued the fourth.

'*Yes*!' screamed the fifth.

'Clock strikes three,' said Oak.

Next were the yews and cypresses, and the voice that sounded in Alan's ear was the dreary voice of Holy Yew.

'We have considered this grave matter carefully,' it said. 'We dislike violence. We seek the ways of peace and brotherhood. But in this case we are persuaded that an example should be made. I myself was rudely insulted by a boy of the human species and when I went out of my way to set him on the right track, he did not so much as thank me. The holy yews and the slim cypresses are of one opinion and our vote is *yes*.'

'*No*,' another voice boomed out.

Alan scanned the company of yews and cypresses to see who had spoken. Right at the back, on his own, was Lord Cedar.

Holy Yew was furious at this interruption.

'With all due respect to Lord Cedar,' he said coldly, 'he chose to remain silent while we deliberated this issue. The yews and cypresses are agreed. Lord Cedar said nothing and he has no right to speak now. We vote *yes*.'

Treetime

'The yew is right,' came the chilly voice of Mister Ash.

'None shall speak but at three of the clock,' said Oak sternly.

'And we vote *yes*,' repeated Holy Yew.

'*No*,' boomed Lord Cedar once more.

'You must give your reasons at least,' said the yew, but Lord Cedar said nothing.

'A blank vote at three of the clock,' ruled Broad Oak.

Alan could see Holy Yew hopping with indignation, but the ruling was made and the vote passed on.

'Clock strikes four,' called Oak.

'We, the limes and beams, wish no harm to mankind. We are of one mind and we vote *no*.'

Two–one, thought Alan, and the yews are out of it.

As he moved to the next window he heard Oak call out number five.

It was the fruit trees and a large apple tree spoke for them.

'We apples and pears and plums and peaches and cherries and apricots and damsons and quinces are of one mind. We vote *no*.'

'So do I,' said another voice.

'Sorry, Fig,' said the apple. 'We apples and pears and plums and cherries and apricots and damsons and quinces and Fig are of one mind. *No.*'

'Now you forgot us,' said a juicy little voice.

'Oh. We apples and pears and plums and peaches and cherries and apricots and damsons and quinces and Fig are of one mind. We vote *no*,' said the apple, getting it right at last.

'Clock strikes six,' said Oak.

It was the turn of Whispering Beech.

'We have all heard the breeze that says soon we will sleep,' came the murmuring, rustling tones of Beech's voice, 'and the beeches feel we should leave this place in peace. And so our vote is *no*.'

We're winning, thought Alan. It was three–two to the Noes.

'Clock strikes seven,' called Broad Oak.

'We have had some trouble reaching our decision,' said the next voice, which Alan saw was Sir Sycamore's. 'But in view of what Beech has just said, I think I can say, not that we are of one mind, because of course we have many minds, many opinions, and everybody who has spoken has been quite right, yet we feel that Beech is the – how shall I put it? – the *rightest*, and the sycamores and maples, on balance, weighing one thing against another and seeing both sides of the question, say *no*.'

'Clock strikes eight,' came Oak's voice.

The nuts were next. Chestnuts and walnuts and hazels and almonds. Their spokesman was a big old horse chestnut of few words.

'The nuts say *no*,' he said.

That made it five–two, but from the next window Alan could see the pines, and next to them were the willows.

'Clock strikes nine.'

The colossal redwood was their spokesman. He had an American accent.

'There's a helluva lot of us guys and we're pretty big and I'm the biggest of all and I figure we should have had two or three votes and not one. There's pines and firs and spruces and larches over here and not least myself. And we're the ones that men hassle most of all. So we say that we break up this little place here and make matchwood of it, and take out its little people and plant them *in rows tied to stakes* and see how they like it. We say *yeah*.'

'Clock strikes ten,' called Oak.

Alan was right about the willows as well. A great white willow lay rather than stood at the head of the tribe, most of the length of its trunk flat along the ground, like a monstrous serpent. Behind stood the other willows, all shapes and sizes, and behind them were the poplars, apparently looking at something far away.

Bugging

'We willows,' began their spokesman in a slow, sinuous voice, 'care little for the doings of men and little enough for the tribes of tree. But the waters of this land have grown sour with the slops of cities and the poisonous slush of farms and we do not like this. If Mister Ash and the buzzing thorns wish to teach a lesson to these careless humans, let them do so. We say *yes*.'

That made it five–four to the Noes. Still to come were the elders, the oaks, the elms and the birches. Alan counted nervously on his fingers. Oak was a No, of course, but the elms and birches were certain Yeses. That would be six-all. So a lot depended on Berry Elder, and he knew it.

'Clock strikes eleven,' said Oak.

Berry Elder puffed himself to his full height before starting. As usual he started off as if he'd been talking already.

'... wonder what to do in a case like this.' His voice trilled breathlessly in Alan's ear. 'We elders are not mighty like the oaks or tall like the beeches and we don't grow to a great age like the yews or get cut about like the thorns in the hedges or sliced into planks like the pines, yet as all of you know we do have our value, being quick and clever and spreading wherever there is room and wherever there is not, and our flowers make champagne and our berries make wine and our

Treetime

wood is supple and our leaves are glossy. We've been here since Roman times and as our name implies...'

'You've a knack for too much talk, Berry Elder. Be quick and take your pick.' Oak's voice.

Alan could tell at once that this was a mistake. It was Berry Elder's great moment, holding the stage at the Great Clock. And here he was, publicly ticked off by Broad Oak.

He was silent for a moment, and when he spoke again it was in quite another fashion.

'Be quick, says Oak! Nobody ever tells Broad Oak to be quick, do they? Nobody tells Broad Oak what to do. We all know, anyway, how Broad Oak will vote, don't we? And we know how the elms and birches will vote, too. So little Berry Elder has the deciding vote, does he not? And little Berry Elder, being of one mind with all his fellow elders,' – here the throng of elders behind him nodded vigorously – 'hereby tells the thorns to *go ahead*. Berry Elder says *yes*.'

A roar of approval went up from the thorns. Alan would have heard it even if it hadn't been transmitted through the extraordinary little radio that sat on his shoulder. But it seemed that neither the daddy-long-legs nor Oak nor anyone else could save the house now.

'No heckling, no clamour,' shouted Oak.

'Clock strikes twelve, and Oak says *no*.'

The small, sad group of elm saplings was next. For a time none of them seemed to want to speak, and Alan watched as one of them was finally pushed forward by its fellows.

'None of us will get to live very long,' said a miserable little voice, 'and we miss our parents and grandparents and all the big folk of our tree tribe. Things will change, Mister Ash told us, if we vote to punish human beings, so we will vote *yes*.'

Last of all were the silver birches. How beautiful they were, with their gleaming white trunks and their rain of tiny leaves! And there among them Alan spotted the little red-and-white caps of the toadstools.

'YES for the dryads,'

sang Silver Birch.

'YES for the old ways,
YES for the pagan days,
YES to marvels, to mushrooms, to magic!'

What followed was very confused. The thorns set up a loud buzzing, Oak was calling for order, and then many voices started shouting something that Alan couldn't hear. Someone had arrived. But who? Silver Birch could be heard calling out

Treetime

indignantly. Then there was a series of fizzing, crackling noises from Daddy-long-legs' channels, and once something like a loud 'pop'.

Then at last Alan could see what the fuss was all about. For between the excited birches and the little group of sad elm saplings, there appeared in the distance a tree, not very tall, not very broad, but with leaves of the deepest and glossiest green of all. It seemed to have great difficulty in staying upright and swayed dangerously from side to side. Every few steps it nearly tripped over its own roots.

'It's Lonely Alder!' cried Alan aloud.

Daddy-long-legs had apparently managed to sort out the problems he was having with his system and Oak's gruff voice came clearly through.

'The Great Clock has *not* completed its last strike. Alder must speak!'

And then the unmistakable sound of Mister Ash: 'Alder was too late, the vote was over, the die is cast, the destruction shall begin!'

The thorns buzzed even louder, Oak boomed out for silence, Ash was still speaking, Big Red's Yankee voice was trying to say something. But Daddy-long-legs was in trouble again and there was another series of crackles and fizzes, and another loud 'pop'.

There was a moment's silence and then a faint

Bugging

humming began and Alan saw the daddy-long-legs' body and wings and antennae vibrate as before. The humming grew louder and then softer, the insect lifted briefly off Alan's shoulder and the daddy-long-legs was back.

'Are you there, Daddy?' asked the boy.

'I'm here.' The little voice sounded even tinier and further away than before.

'What's the matter with you. I can hardly hear you.'

'I'm tired.'

'Oh, is that all? That's all right then.'

'I'm *very* tired.'

Something in the tiny voice made Alan anxious.

'You're not ill, are you?'

'I think . . . I may have . . . slightly . . . exhausted . . . my systems,' the daddy-long-legs whispered.

'Rest then. Lie down somewhere. You'll be OK.'

'Put me down . . . somewhere quiet . . . I can't manage . . . flying.'

'Of course I will, Daddy. Don't you worry, you'll be right as rain in a minute.'

'What did you say?'

'You'll be right as rain in a minute.'

'I can't hear you . . . Did you say something?'

Alan forgot about the alders and the vote. His little friend was ill.

He picked him off his shoulder as gently as he could between his thumb and forefinger. But it wasn't gentle enough.

'Ow!' said the tiny voice, and the long delicate wings whirred into life as the daddy-long-legs made his last flight. He lifted out of Alan's grasp, up a little way, and then his balance seemed to go, the wings folded and he spun slowly to the ground like a feather.

For a moment Alan couldn't see where he had landed. When he found him, tears started to his eyes. The daddy-long-legs was on his back, legs in the air and sort of folded up.

The boy didn't dare use his fingers to pick him up again and risk hurting him. He found a piece of card from his desk and bent down to try and slide it carefully under the insect's body. As he did so he could just hear the feeble voice.

'Are you there, Alan?' it enquired faintly.

'I'm here,' Alan shouted.

'No? Oh well. He's gone. He's gone and I'm gone and it's all going.'

The voice grew thinner and thinner as if disappearing into an endless void. Alan was on his hands and knees with his ear as close to the daddy-long-legs as he could get it.

'Too much power . . . too many circuits . . . burned out . . . can't hear now . . . but what's

Bugging

that? Ahh! Music . . . it's music . . . it's music . . . it's music.'

The voice faded away; the daddy-long-legs' body gave a little twitch and was still.

Alan felt a sob rising inside him, but he wouldn't cry. No, he would not. It was all Ash's fault. It was Mister Ash who was to blame for all this. Well, he'd show him.

He fought back his tears and raced out of the room and down the stairs.

14 The Attack

Alan had no idea what he was going to do as he hurtled out of the house. Perhaps he thought he would simply attack Mister Ash with his fists.

There in a circle stood Broad Oak, Mister Ash, Silver Birch and the huge redwood, and there was a heated argument going on. Out of the corner of his eye, Alan saw a horde of thorns buzzing furiously just behind Silver Birch.

To get to Oak, Alan had to run right underneath the redwood. Not that there was much danger – Big Red's lowest branches were far above the boy's head.

'What's this?' Big Red bellowed as Alan shot past him.

'Jack's with me,' said Oak firmly.

The boy ran up to him.

'Climb up if you like,' said Oak.

'I'll stay here,' said the boy, and stood with one hand resting on Oak's knotty trunk.

'A *boy* at the Great Clock!' boomed Redwood. 'Send him home!'

Redwood's words resounded round the clearing and the cry was echoed by other voices

The Attack

among the tribes.

'But this *is* my home,' Alan said at the top of his voice. 'I live here and I've been listening to all of you planning to destroy my house, just because the elms have gone, and it's wrong because humans are sad about the elms, too. It was a beetle that did it, not people. A beetle gave them a disease and people wanted to save the elms. I know because they told us at school. They cut down the elms because they're trying to get rid of the disease, not because they don't like them. And now Daddy-long-legs has died, and anyway what will happen to my mum and Emily if you break up the house? It's not fair, and it's not really about the elms at all; it's because Mister Ash hates the swing and the house and he's to blame for everything.'

While Alan was speaking, all in a rush to say everything that was on his mind, the other trees had broken ranks and drawn closer. The Great Clock gradually disappeared and what was left was like a dense forest of trees of every kind, with one small clearing at the centre where there stood a small cottage and a small boy talking to a small audience of tremendous trees.

Alan's words could only be heard by Oak, Ash, Birch and Redwood, but they were carried by the murmuring breeze that had impressed the daddy-

Treetime

long-legs, until even the trees furthest away had been told what the boy had said. Daddy-long-legs would not have been quite so impressed if he had heard the following conversation.

'What's going on?' asked one small plum tree on the very edge of things who could neither hear nor see a thing.

'The daddy-big-leg killed the elms and Mister Ash is really to blame,' said a nearby apricot.

'Oh,' said the small plum as if that explained the whole thing.

Lonely Alder arrived at the clearing at last, hobbling slowly along. Broad Oak moved to one side to make room for him.

'Welcome to the Great Clock, Alder,' he said. 'Lucky you came.'

'I know I'm a little late,' said Alder pleasantly, 'and if I hadn't happened to meet this young man, I would never have stirred from the river bank. Alders don't care for politics and Clocks and talk. In fact if my branches had made better paddles, I wouldn't be here. But since I am here, it's obvious to everyone that I have as much right to vote as anybody else. Alders were here before oaks and before ashes. We are as old as elms in this land. And as some of you may know, Birch and I are cousins. We are of the same tribe, Birch and I, so we share a vote at fourteen of the

Clock. Isn't that so, Birch?'

'Late or early, right or wrong,
The only song now is the birch's song.
Who is the oldest, you or I,
Which came first, the earth or the sky?
If the alder finds words, then we shall take note,
But if he stays silent, why how can he vote?'

As before, all the trees fell silent when Birch spoke, and a sleepy, dreamy feeling fell over the whole gathering. Alan was trying to work out what Birch was saying. Of course Alder wouldn't stay silent. Of course he would vote to save the house. But when the boy looked towards Lonely Alder, he saw that the dreaded toadstools had crept up from behind him and made their terrible ring.

'Sneaky Birch!' thundered Oak. 'Call off your tricky folk!'

But Silver Birch just laughed silkily and began a little dance of triumph.

'That's that, then,' said Mister Ash. 'Come on, Redwood, take the roof off.'

But to everyone's astonishment, that was not quite that. For the next to speak was Lonely Alder.

'As I was saying,' he continued, as if nothing

had happened. 'We are as old as the elms and as old as the birches, and my dear cousin seems to have forgotten that these conjuring tricks of hers don't much bother the likes of me. If I can find words, she said, then she will take note. So take note all of you. There's something about a home, whether it be a house made of bricks or a nest made of twigs or a burrow dug in the earth or, as in my case, a fold in a bank by the river, that should be sacred to all. It's true that men have gone too far. They are poisoning the waters, the willows say, and poisoning the air too, so my leaves tell me. There is too much chopping and clearing and trimming. Perhaps they should be taught a lesson. But destroying homes is not the right way, and my vote is *no*!'

'The Great Clock has struck,' Oak declared firmly. 'Six Noes, six Yeses and two *blanks*.' The way he said 'blanks' made it sound like the last possible word on the matter.

There was some cheering at this, and some booing too, but nobody spoke up against it, not even Silver Birch or Mister Ash. In fact Alan noticed that Mister Ash was no longer in his place at the edge of the clearing.

It seemed that most of the trees agreed with what Alder had said and many of them began moving off to where they had come from. Alan

The Attack

went up to Alder and thanked him.

'Don't mention it,' said Alder. 'I had the best trip of my life – the only trip of my life, I should say – because of you. Don't forget to come and visit me. I've got to go now. I've been away from the river far too long already.'

Alder set off in his own precarious way, and Alan looked round to see the slopes around his house filled with trees, alone or in groups, making their way homeward.

'That's that, Jack,' said Broad Oak. 'Time to make tracks. We were lucky to keep them from wrecking your shack.'

But at that moment there was a crash from the other side of the house.

Alan rushed round the corner of the building and ran slap into a bunch of angry thorns. Beyond them were more, and much taller, thorns, and beyond them stood Mister Ash in his usual position by the side of the house. Next to him was Silver Birch.

'Catch the boy!' shouted Mister Ash.

But there was no need for Mister Ash's command, for Alan was already caught. Two of the thorns had closed round him and he stood in a tangle of thorny branches from which there was no escape.

The crash he had heard was a piece of guttering and some roof tiles that were the first victims of the thorns' assault on the house. Behind and above them stood Big Red. The top of him was bending slightly towards the roof of the house, and his lower branches were reaching down towards it.

'Danged if the thing isn't too low for me,' he grunted. He tried swaying his top backwards and then swooping forward again, but still his branches only clutched at thin air a few metres above the chimney.

'Get on with it,' said Mister Ash to the thorns impatiently. 'There's not much time. Break the place up and get back to your hedges and thickets before the Big Sleep starts.'

Neither Mister Ash nor Silver Birch took part in the attack themselves, but both were urging on the thorns in their work of destruction. A loud smash told Alan that one of the kitchen windows had gone, and more tiles fell from the roof.

Broad Oak appeared round the corner of the house and he was very angry.

'I'll knock you over and crack your necks and break you into sticks!' he shouted.

The thorns scuttled back from the house at his appearance. Big Red was in the middle of swaying back as far as he could go to launch his next attempt at the roof, and Oak reached out a branch and gave him one sharp smack high up on

his trunk that all but toppled him completely. Big Red's roots scrabbled desperately backwards to prevent the disaster, but the mighty trunk was still leaning at a dangerous angle to the ground.

'Whoooah!' Big Red yelled.

He couldn't get his trunk upright again. His roots ran faster and faster to try and get underneath him, and Alan watched him being carried further and further from the house. Oak turned his attention to Mister Ash and Silver Birch.

'It's not for you to make the laws,'

chanted Birch,

'There are older rules by far than yours.'

'The Clock makes the laws,' said Oak, 'and you've broken them. Go back home quick, for your own sake.'

Mister Ash chuckled his chilly chuckle.

'I am at home, Broad Oak; it is you who are still far from where you live. As for the thorns, they live in the hedge, just over there. It is you, Thick Oak, who will be caught by the Big Sleep. Your roots will try to burrow into the earth, but they will wither in the winter and your boughs will grow brittle one by one. Next spring, when I and Birch and the thorns are green once more, we will watch you slowly rot.'

The Attack

Broad Oak was silenced for a moment, thinking on this grim fate. Alan wondered how soon the Big Sleep would start. All the other trees had now gone home. Even most of the thorns were traipsing quietly back to their places in the hedges and thickets at the end of the garden. In the big meadow beyond, Big Red could still be seen, running first one way and then the other, with his colossal trunk swaying dangerously to and fro. As Alan watched him, he finally managed to regain his balance and began stalking off up the hill.

Only Mister Ash, Silver Birch, Broad Oak and a few of the thorns, including the ones that had hold of Alan, remained by the house.

Silver Birch now spoke.

> *'The Sleep draws near, but I have no fear,*
> *For my home is close and my speed is swift.*
> *And for you, Broad Oak, and for all your*
>   *folk,*
> *I leave you a parting gift.'*

With this, she shook her myriad leaves, sprang nimbly to the corner of the wall and vanished behind the house.

Alan fought to free himself from the clutches of the two thorns but he was caught fast. He knew immediately what Silver Birch's parting gift would be, but Broad Oak apparently did not.

Treetime

So, as Oak moved heavily up to where Ash stood, he didn't notice a line of silent toadstools marching round the corner of the house where Silver Birch had just disappeared.

'I'll take you with me, Bleak Ash,' growled Oak.

His great branches smacked a couple of thorns out of the way and stretched out towards Mister Ash. Mister Ash's own branches came out to stop Broad Oak's advance but these, too, were swept aside. There was a sound of cracking as Oak closed in, and his longest boughs, longer by far than anything that Mister Ash possessed, reached round Ash's trunk and began pulling him from his spot.

'Look out for the toadstools, Broad Oak,' Alan yelled.

The oak didn't even hear, but the toadstools did, and they recognized the voice of the goal-kicker. Twice he had escaped from them, but here he was again, and this time he couldn't get away. Their line of march turned away from Broad Oak and towards the boy.

Oak could not, after all, pull Mister Ash away. Already the ash's roots had taken hold and it was too much even for Oak's massive strength.

As he tugged, Oak felt the first tide of the Big Sleep wash over him. Reluctantly he let go of the

The Attack

ash and turned slowly away. Now he had only one thought, to get home while he still could.

'I will not kip and I will not tucker,' he murmured to himself. 'I must keep awake.'

So he never saw the toadstools make their ring around Alan. He never saw the two thorns let go of the boy and stumble dizzily off towards their places in the hedge. And he never saw the boy himself run vainly round and round the spinning toadstool spell before falling in a heap at its centre.

Afterword

When Treetime was over, the night came back, and six hours later the real dawn came.

'How could I have slept through a storm like that?' Alan's mother asked herself as she looked sleepily out of the kitchen window.

Bits of guttering and a number of roof tiles lay strewn around the garden. Glass from the broken window was all over the kitchen floor. Twigs and small branches littered the ground at the foot of the ash tree, and the ash itself seemed to have been bent. One of its larger branches was split down the middle.

What a wind to do all that! thought Alan's mum.

At this moment she heard someone fiddling with the latch of the outside door.

'Who's there?' she said, alarmed.

The door opened and there stood her son.

You can imagine what a sight he was. Pale, plastered in mud, scratched and stung, with his tracksuit in tatters and a dazed look in his eye.

And you can imagine the fuss that followed. Towels and hot drinks and dry clothes and extra

Afterword

sweaters and plenty of scolding.

'Fancy going outside on a night like that! The boy has no brain. It's a wonder he didn't catch his death.' And so on, and so on, in the way that mothers will.

The stove was lit, even though it was summer, and Alan was put in the rocking chair beside it, covered in blankets, and ordered to drink mugs of hot tea.

Gradually his eyes lost their dazed look and some colour returned to his cheeks.

'Well, you look a bit better, but what *have* you been up to?' said his mother. She fussed with his blankets for the umpteenth time. She was still anxious, for the boy hadn't yet said a word. She knelt beside him and took his hand.

'Aren't you going to tell me what happened?' she said.

'I've got to go out,' he said suddenly.

'You are going nowhere but to bed, young fellow,' she said firmly. 'Out, indeed!'

'You see, I've got to go and see if Broad Oak made it back.'

It made no sense to her. Nor any of the things he said, about red and white toadstools and someone called Mister Ash.

'You've had a terrible nightmare, my lad.'

It was the only explanation. Such a bad nightmare, apparently, that he'd been sleepwalking too. Sleepwalking, sleepfighting and sleepswimming as well, by the look of him. But for the moment she said nothing of all that.

But he knew it hadn't been a dream. He knew by the guttering and the tiles in the garden. He knew by the broken window-pane and the state of his tracksuit which lay in a bundle in the corner of the kitchen. Abruptly, he sprang to his feet and dashed upstairs, his mother hard on his heels.

'A broken pane up here as well,' she said crossly as they entered the attic.

But Alan wasn't interested in the broken pane. He was on his hands and knees under the opposite window. After a moment he found what he was looking for.

'What on earth are you up to, Alan? What *have* you got there?'

Alan cradled the lifeless daddy-long-legs gently in his hands.

'You shouldn't have tried it, Daddy,' he said. 'It was too much for you. Why didn't you just tell me what they were saying?'

He felt himself wanting to cry again.

His mother went to phone the doctor.

'You're the cleverest, cleverest bug in the world,' said Alan.

The doctor came and went. Medicines were

Afterword

prescribed and complete rest was ordered. Emily got up late and was intrigued by all the fuss. It was she, and not her mother, who got to hear the whole story.

'So we've got to go and see if Broad Oak made it home,' Alan finished.

'Of course we have,' said Emily sensibly.

'But we'll have to slip out without Mum knowing.'

As it happened, Mum made it easy for them. She tucked Alan up in bed, put Emily to watch over him and slipped out on her bike to get the pills from the chemist.

'And you make sure that he doesn't move from his bed, Emily,' she said before she left.

'OK, Mum,' said Emily. But she had her fingers crossed behind her back.

No sooner had the bicycle disappeared up the track than the children were out of the back door.

'Look, there are the toadstools still there,' said Alan. 'And see how Mister Ash is bent where Oak got him.'

'We'll have to get the swing tied up again,' said Emily.

'I don't think so, Em. I think we'd better move it altogether. The swing was really the start of the whole thing, you know.'

'But we must have a swing!'

Treetime

'Yes, but we'll find a nice oak or a beech for it.'
'OK then.'

They hurried out over the meadow, circled the Toot and came to the edge of the wood where Broad Oak lived.

Long before they got there, they could see the old tree had indeed survived his sleepy journey home. There he was, as always, strong and peaceful, a breeze just stirring his leaves.

'Let's climb up,' said Alan.

'It looks rather difficult,' Emily said.

'No. It's easy. There are cracks and knuckles and kinks at the back.'

And there were.

More About Trees

Here are descriptions of some of the trees you have just read about in *Treetime*:

Ash Ash is a tall tree (it can grow up to 45 m) with a fairly slender trunk (up to 6.7 m round). The bark is ash-grey, smooth on young trees but ridged on older ones. Its feathery leaves have about seven sets of oval leaflets arranged opposite each other with one at the top. The edges of the leaflets have short teeth. Ash has distinctive seeds known as keys which hang in bunches. It is a short-lived tree, surviving up to 150 years.

Beech Sometimes called 'the Lady of the Woods', beech has a tall, straight trunk and a spreading network of fine branches. The roots do not grow deeply and can often be seen spreading from the trunk. It is a slow-growing tree of great size (up to 43 m tall and 8 m round), but it seldom lives for longer than 200 years. Beech has a smooth metallic-grey bark. The leaves are oval with a wavy edge, a short stalk and a pointed tip. They are very smooth and shiny on top. Beech

More About Trees

nuts grow inside small prickly cases.

Cedar (of Lebanon) Cedar has a massive trunk with large spreading branches which grow horizontally to form table-like masses of needles. It can grow up to 40 m high. The bark is smooth and green at first but becomes brown, scaly and furrowed with age. Cedar is an evergreen with egg-shaped cones which seem smooth when green because the scales overlap so tightly. They turn brown as they ripen and break up while they still on the tree, so you won't find them on the ground beneath it.

Elder Elder is usually no more than a bush, but it sometimes forms a small tree. The bark of young stems is pale yellowish-brown, but on older wood it is greyish-brown, thick, furrowed and corky. The elder blossoms in June and the tiny fragrant white blossoms become small, juicy, purple-black elderberries.

Elm Elms have been severely threatened by the spread of Dutch Elm disease in the past few years. They are fast-growing, very tall trees (up to 45 m high), with broad trunks (up to 8 m round). The crown usually separates into two, three or four tiers. The rough grey-brown bark is broken into squarish plates. Its leaves are oval-shaped with

Treetime

teeth around the edge, and a pointed tip.

Oak A big, fine tree, up to 37 m tall and 9 m round the trunk. Look for a wide strong trunk with a widely spaced and much-branched crown of a rounded shape. It has rough grey bark with many small cracks and deep grooves. The leaves have rounded lobes growing from a long rib in the centre, and untoothed edges. A slow-growing, long-living tree, it can stand for over 1000 years.

Silver Birch Never a very large tree (reaching at most about 26m tall) and with a slender trunk (up to 3.7 m round), silver birch has a beautiful white bark that peels off in strips as the tree grows. Older trees have wrinkles of black bark up the trunk. The branches tend to be shortish, slender and flexible. The leaves are triangular, oval or diamond-shaped with toothed edges, ending in a pointed tip.

Sycamore A quick-growing, large tree, sycamore can reach 38 m in height and up to 6.7 m around the middle. It has thick branches with a dense cover of leaves. The bark is smooth and purplish-grey. The leaves have long, reddish stalks and are hand-shaped, with five rounded 'fingers'. The seeds are winged and twirl in the breeze like helicopter blades.

More About Trees

Thorn Thorns are usually hedgerow plants, but they can grow into a small tree. Hawthorn has short spines on its zig-zag shoots and its bark is greyish-green. It produces white blossom in May which becomes scarlet fruit in the autumn. Blackthorn has black bark with thorn-studded twigs, and dark green oval leaves. It produces star-shaped white blossom in April. Its fruit, called sloes, are round and purplish-black with a bluish-white bloom.

Yew Often found in churchyards, yew has a short trunk, a thick cover of branches and leaves and, in late summer, cones which look like red berries. The leaves and the seeds are poisonous. The trunk is light brown, leaving reddish patches where it flakes. The leaves are flat pointed needles, glossy on top and pale green beneath. Yew can live to a great age, perhaps for 1,000 years.

Glossary

clamour (p. 21) – a loud, continuous, confused noise or shouting; a loud strong demand or complaint
copse (p. 26) – a wood of small growth where the trees are regularly cut (called coppicing)
dell (p. 26) – a deep hollow or small valley with grass, usually covered with trees
dryad (p. 26) – from Ancient Greek myths, a spirit who lived in a tree and whose life ended with the death of the tree
fornicate (p. 33) – to have sexual relations with someone outside marriage
grove (p. 26) – a group of trees, planted or natural; an avenue of trees; a wood of small size
haphazardly (p. 93) – in an unplanned, disorderly manner
lugubrious (p. 80) – mournful, dismal
menagerie (p. 1) – a collection of wild animals held in captivity either privately or in a public place
nymph (p. 26) – from Greek and Roman myths – goddesses of nature, who lived in trees, streams, and mountains
obscurely (p. 64) – in a hard to understand, unclear way
precarious (p. 121) – unsafe, not firm or steady
sinuous (p. 109) – twisting like a snake; full of curves
spinney (p. 26) – a small area full of trees and low plants
superstitious (p. 61) – full of beliefs not based on reason or fact; believing in the supernatural, omens, magic, etc.
thicket (p. 26) – a dense mass of trees or shrubs
vicinity (p. 20) – the surrounding area